D0746808

"You know, my dear," he said, keeping his voice low, "if you have trouble meeting the obligation, I am sure we could find some mutually satisfying way of settling accounts."

There was that wide-eyed stare of muddled incomprehension. Miss Lattimore hadn't the faintest idea of what he was shamefully suggesting. So he showed her; he'd wanted to kiss her since she lifted the veil—he placed his lips on hers and kissed her.

Sydney struggled and he released her immediately. Smiling.

"You . . . you," she sputtered. "You were right. Moneylenders are vermin." And she slapped him.

Also by Barbara Metzger:

MY LADY INNKEEPER*
EARLY ENGAGEMENT*
CUPBOARD KISSES*
BETHING'S FOLLY
THE EARL AND THE HEIRESS
RAKE'S RANSOM
MINOR INDISCRETIONS*
THE LUCK OF THE DEVIL*

*Published by Fawcett Books

AN
AFFAIR
OF
INTEREST

Barbara Metzger

FAWCETT CREST • NEW YORK

Sale of this book without a front cover may be unauthorized. If this book is coverless, it may have been reported to the publisher as "unsold or destroyed" and neither the author nor the publisher may have received payment for it.

A Fawcett Crest Book
Published by Ballantine Books
Copyright © 1991 by Barbara Metzger

All rights reserved under International and Pan-American Copyright Conventions. Published in the United States by Ballantine Books, a division of Random House, Inc., New York, and simultaneously in Canada by Random House of Canada Limited, Toronto.

Library of Congress Catalog Card Number: 91-92205

ISBN 0-449-21874-0

Manufactured in the United States of America

First Edition: January 1992

This one's for craft-show friends,
creative, talented, and *nice* people,
especially Barb, John, Russ and Debbie.

1

Money and Matrimony

If love were a loaf of bread, the Lattimore sisters could afford the crust, or perhaps a handful of crumbs. Being one half-pay pension away from poverty, neither Miss Winifred Lattimore nor her younger sister Sydney could afford the luxury of love in a cottage, not when their own cottage needed a new roof. One of them, at least, had to find a wealthy husband.

"But why must it be me?" Winifred poked at the tangled skeins of needlework in her lap. The discussion had been going on for some time, to Miss Lattimore's obvious distress. The needlepoint armrest was not faring much better.

"Why, you are the oldest, Winnie. Of course you must marry first," her sister answered, rescuing the knotted yarns from further mayhem. Heaven knew they needed the new armcover. Sydney plunked herself down in a patch of sun by her grandfather's chair and straightened the blanket over the general's knees before starting to unravel the mess. "Am I not right, Grandfather?"

General Harlan Lattimore, retired, raised one blue-veined, trembling hand to where his youngest granddaughter's single long braid shone red-gold in the sun. He patted her head as if to say she was a good girl, and grunted.

Sydney took that for assent. "You see, Winnie, the general agrees. Gracious, you are twenty years old already. You are like to dwindle into an old maid here in Little Dedham, while I am only eighteen and have ages left before I need think of putting on my caps. Besides, you are prettier."

The general grunted again. He didn't have to agree quite so quickly, Sydney thought, for all it was the truth. Winnie had the fragile blond-haired, blue-eyed beauty so eternally admired, an elegant carriage, the fairest of complexions, and a smile that could have graced a medieval Madonna. Her hair even fell in perfect ringlets from a ribbon-tied twist atop her perfectly formed head. Sydney scowled at the snarled yarns in her lap, considering her own impossible gingery mop that refused to take a curl no matter how many uncomfortable nights she spent in papers. Of course, it had to be matched with a tendency to freckles, she continued her honest appraisal, and nondescript hazel eyes, a complexion more sun-browned than any lady should permit, and a body more sturdy than willowy. No, Winnie stood a much better chance of landing them a nabob. If only she would try.

"You are much more the domestic type anyway, Winnie, teaching Sunday school, visiting the parish poor. You know you couldn't wait for Clara

Bristowe to have her new baby so you could hold him."

"Yes, but a rich man with a big fancy house." Winnie fussed with the ribbons of her sash. "I don't know, Sydney. You are a much better manager than I. Think how you have been taking care of us since Mama passed on."

The general nodded. Sydney had done a good job, or at least the best she could, holding household on what His Majesty's government saw fit to award its retired officers. Mama's annuity had expired with her three years earlier, along with her widow's benefits from Papa's military unit. Since the general's seizure shortly after, Sydney had been juggling their meager finances to maintain both the cottage and Grandfather's comfort with just Mrs. Minch as housekeeper and his ex-batman Griffith as man-of-all-work.

"Exactly, Winnie," Sydney declared proudly. The pride may have more to do with unknotting a particularly tangled skein than her accomplishments as a frugal chatelaine. That last particular skill was one she was hoping to find unnecessary in the future. "And that's precisely why we should bend our efforts to finding you a husband. No man wants a managing-type female, Winnie, they want a sweet, gentle girl." She smiled up at her sister, showing her dimples and her love. "And no one is sweeter or more lovely than you, dearest. Any man would be fortunate to win you for his bride."

Winnie blushed, and the general grunted his concurrence. Then he stroked his other granddaughter's head again and said, "Aargh."

Sydney covered his gnarled hand with her own.

"Yes, Grandfather, I know you are fond of me too, even if I am no biddable miss. We'll come about."

The old man smiled, and Sydney couldn't help feeling a trifle guilty that she liked him so much better now than she did when he had all his faculties. He'd made their lives hell, and Mama's, too, before she died, running the house like a military installation. The general had to have the best of everything—food, wine, horseflesh—and instant obedience to his every whim. He issued orders to family, neighbors, and servants alike until no one in the village would work for them and none of their friends would come to call. One day he'd thrown an apoplectic fit over some sheep in his path, falling off his horse into the street. The local men waited a good long while, making sure he wouldn't lay into them with his riding crop, before they picked up the general and carried him home. He had not walked since, nor spoken. For the most part, the Lattimore home was a great deal more peaceful.

The general seemed resigned to his Bath chair, napping in the sun, having his granddaughters read the war news to him, listening to the clacking of the village hens when they came to call, bearing gossip and sharing their good cooking. He'd led a long life, called his own tunes. Now it was time to pass on the command before sounding retreat. But he was worried.

When the general fretted, life in the cottage resembled an army camp under siege. All the other nodcocks rushed around, bringing him things he wouldn't have wanted if he were in his prime. That pretty widgeon of a granddaughter even started blubbering when she couldn't understand the general's agitation. If there was anything General

4

Lattimore couldn't abide, it was a spineless subaltern. Even his man Griffith took to acting out charades as if the general were deaf, blast him. Only Sydney seemed to understand. Too bad she wasn't a lad, the general thought. She'd have made a deuced fine aide-de-camp.

He'd no more leave his men in the field without ammunition than he'd let his family be thrown out in the cold. But, damn, his pension wouldn't last forever. Hell, not even General Harlan Lattimore thought he'd last forever. Of course Sydney knew what worried him; she was worried, too. That's why they were having this discussion, to convince Winnie that she had to make a marriage of convenience, for all of their sakes.

Winifred wiped her eyes with a mangled scrap of lace. "But, but, Sydney, what if I cannot like him?"

Sydney jumped up, tossing the yarns into an even worse pile. "Silly goose," she said, hugging her sister, "that's the best part. I'm fussy and crabby, but you like everybody!"

The next question, naturally, was where to find the paragon good enough for their Winnie. He first had to be rich, but Sydney vowed she would insist on a cultured gentleman. She was not tossing her gentle sister to any caper-merchant hoping to better his standing in the social world. He should be handsome, too, this husband Winnie would be facing over the breakfast dishes for the rest of her life. And kind, Winnie put in. Most of all, he had to be generous enough to accept a bride with a houseful of dependents and a dowry slightly better than that of a milkmaid.

The answer to the question of locating this most

eligible of *partis* was, of course, London. He could be lurking anywhere, in truth, anywhere but Little Dedham, that is, since the local bachelors—sheep farmers, squires' sons, tutors, and linen-drapers— had been coming round the cottage for years. None had fulfilled Winifred's romantic dreams or Sydney's mercenary ones.

Winnie laughed, a gay, tinkling sound. "London, Sydney? Now who is dreaming? You know Aunt Harriet would never invite us."

"And I shan't ask her, the old cat!" Sydney did not look the least contrite, speaking thus of their maternal relation, not even at her sister's gasp. "Well, you know it's true, Winnie. Telling us the strain of Cousin Trixie's come-out was too much for her to undertake presenting another debutante! It's not as if she doesn't still have that platter-faced chit on her hands this Season, and dragging two girls from party to party cannot be any more exhausting than one. Before that it was firing off Cousin Sophy, or measles in the nursery party, or the general's ill health, though why she thought two of us were required to attend Grandfather at home is beyond me. You could have gone anytime these past years if she weren't afraid of your casting Trixie in the shade."

"She did invite us to Sophy's wedding," Winifred put forth, trying to be fair.

"Yes, and sat you with that tongue-tied young curate for both the dinner before and the breakfast after."

"He was very shy."

"He was poorer than his own church mice, and had less countenance! That was better than my treatment, at any rate. I got put in charge of cataloguing the wedding gifts, for Sophy's thank-yous."

"Aunt knows how very organized and capable you are, dearest," Winnie said, her soft tones trying to soothe her sister's indignation.

It did not work. Sydney had been seething for years over Lady Harriet Windham's slights to her family. "Aunt Harriet knows how to get the most from unpaid servants."

"But you couldn't join the company, Syd, you were not out yet."

"And never will be if left to Aunt Harriet." Sydney took to striding around the small parlor. Winifred hastily wheeled the general into a corner, out of the younger girl's way. "Face it, Winnie, getting blood from a stone would be easier than wringing the least drop of human kindness from Aunt Harriet, and getting her to part with a brass farthing on our behalf would be even harder, the old nipcheese."

"Sydney!" Winifred's scold was drowned out by the general's chuckle. He'd never liked Lady Harriet Windham either, and he wasn't even related to the harpy. She was connected to the girls by marriage, and it was a marriage of which she had never approved. Lord Windham's younger sister Elizabeth's running off to follow the drum with a lieutenant in the Dragoons did not suit her notions of proper behavior. Geoffrey Lattimore's leaving Elizabeth a widow with two small girls and no money suited her even less. Lord Windham's own demise saw the end of any but the most grudging assistance from that quarter, and good riddance, the general thought at the time. Lattimore was a fine old name, with a tradition of serving King and country for generations. There was no getting around the fact, though, that nary a Lattimore put any effort into settling on the land or gathering a fortune or making friends in high places. The Windhams had, blast the parsimonious old trout. The general banged his fist on the chair's armrest. That's why they needed so many new covers.

Sydney retrieved the needlework and set to untangling the mess again. She smiled sunnily at her family, the angry storm over as quickly as it had come. "I have a plan," she announced.

Winnie groaned, but her sister ignored her.

"I do. We're going to London on our own. We'll rent a house of our own and make connections of our own. We won't ask Aunt Harriet, so she cannot say us nay. Once we are there, she shall have to introduce us around, of course, and at least invite us to Trixie's ball. She'd look no-account to her friends in the ton if she ignored her own relatives, and you know how much appearances count to Aunt Harriet. Besides, perhaps she'll feel more kindly to us when she sees we don't mean to hang on her coatsleeves or ask for money."

Winnie's pretty brows were knitted in doubt. "But, Sydney, if we don't ask her for the money, however shall we go?"

Sydney kept her eyes on the embroidery and mumbled something.

The general made noises in his throat, and Winnie asked, "What was that, dear?"

"I said, I have been saving money from the household accounts for a year now." She hurried on. The general had always said to get over rough ground as quickly as possible. "Yes, from our dress allowance." Winnie fingered the skirt of her sprigged muslin gown washed so many times no one could recall what color the little flowers had been. She hadn't had a new dress since—

The general was sounding like a dog with a bone in its mouth, faced with a bigger dog. "And your wines, Grandfather. You know the doctor said spirits were no good for your health. Furthermore, all the port and cognac and fancy brandies you used to drink are being smuggled into the country without excise stamps. You yourself used to say how that was sending money straight to Napoleon to use against our troops."

Winnie's rosebud mouth hung open to think of her sister's daring. Still, a few dress lengths, some bottles of wine, fewer fires, and less candles could never see their way through a Season. She started to speak, but Sydney was already continuing.

"You know how Mama always said I had a good head for figures? Well, I started helping old Mr. Finkle keep track of his profits from the sheep shearing after his boy moved away, in exchange for mutton. Then some of the other sheepherders asked me to help them figure expenses and such, so they wouldn't be cheated when they got to market. They started setting aside a tiny portion from each sale, a lamb here, a ewe pelt there. Now I have a tidy sum in the bank, enough to rent us a modest house. I know, for I've been checking the London papers' advertisements."

Winifred had no head for figures whatsoever. The general did; he shook his head angrily. It wasn't enough blunt by half.

"I know, but there's more. I didn't want to say anything until I was sure, but the Clarkes' daughter-in-law is increasing again, and there's no room down at the mill. They are building a house, but they have agreed to rent our cottage for a few months until it's ready. So we have all that, and Grandfather's pension . . . and my dowry."

The general almost tore the arm off the chair with his good right hand and Winnie cried out, "Oh, no!"

Sydney stood, tossed her thick braid over her shoulder, and crossed her arms, looking like a small, defiant warrior-goddess from some heathen mythology. "Why not? That pittance won't do me any good in Little Dedham, for I *won't* marry a man who cannot add his columns."

"What about Mr. Milke? You know he has always admired you."

"The apothecary?" Sydney grimaced. "He's already supporting his invalidish mother. Besides, he smells of the shop. No, I don't mean to be a snob. He truly does, smell of the shop, that is. Asafoetida drops and camphor and oil of this and tincture of that. I cannot stand next to the man without thinking of *Macbeth*'s witches."

Winifred smiled, as Sydney knew she would. "Very well," Winnie said, "then we'll use my dowry, too." The idea was instantly overthrown.

"No," Sydney insisted, "you shan't go to your handsome hero as any beggar maid. We Lattimores have our pride too. And you must not worry, nor you either, Grandfather. Winnie is sure to attract the finest, most well-to-pass gentleman in all of London! He'll be so smitten, he's bound to open his wine cellars to you and his pockets to me. I'll be so well-dowered, I'll have to watch out for fortune hunters."

And then, Sydney said, but only to herself, she could even marry a poor man if she loved him. Winnie would make a grand marriage, but Sydney vowed she'd become a paid housekeeper rather than wed without love.

Winnie was dancing around the room, wheeling the general's chair to an imaginary waltz. They would get to London after all, with parties and pretty gowns and handsome beaux. Sydney could do anything!

Sydney could do *almost* everything. She could outfit her housekeeper's twin sons, the Minch boys, as footmen and send them off to London to find lodgings. She could move the family, bag and baggage and grouchy general, to the perfect little house on Park Lane. They were on the fringes of Mayfair, but still thoroughly respectable. She could even face down Aunt Harriet, managing to convince that imposing dowager that the Lattimore sisters would be an asset: as eligible men flocked toward Winifred's beauty, they were bound to notice Trixie's . . . ? What? The girl had no charms to recommend her. Lady Windham saw only what she wanted to see though, and was sure the town beaux would recognize her Beatrix's better breeding, especially when compared to Sydney's harum-scarum ways. The rackety gel even refused to wear corsets!

Sydney actually did the near impossible. She improved Trixie's personality, if only by example, showing the browbeaten chit that lightning wouldn't blast from the sky if Mama was contradicted. Trixie blossomed, if one could consider a horse laugh better than a genteel, coy simper.

What Sydney could not do, unfortunately, was make a pence into a pound, nor make one shilling do the work of five or ten. London was expensive. No matter how she figured, no matter how many lists she made or corners she cut, there was not enough money.

They had small expenses, like having calling cards printed, and subscribing to the fashion journals so they could study the latest styles. And medium expenses, like purchasing fine wines to offer the gentlemen who began to call, renting opera boxes, and hiring hackney carriages. In Little Dedham one could walk everywhere. And there were big expenses Sydney had not counted on, like all the dresses considered *de rigueur* for a London miss. She had figured on a new wardrobe for Winnie but, never having been through a London Season, Sydney had not realized exactly how many different functions a popular young lady—and her sister, at Winnie's insistence—was expected to attend. It would not do to wear the same gown too often either.

Sydney certainly never anticipated her own need for fashionable ensembles, nor that she would ever be too busy to sew her own gowns, as she and Winnie had done their entire lives. She surely never budgeted for an abigail to take care of their burgeoning wardrobes. And there was Aunt Harriet, yammering on about Sydney employing a paid companion to act as chaperone for the girls, as if the general and their devoted Minch-brother footmen were not enough protection—or expense.

But it was worth every groat. Sydney was thrilled at the feel of silks and fine muslins and, best of all, Winifred had caught the eye of Baron Scoville. He was perfect for Winnie, pleasant-featured, always courteous, well-respected in the ton, of an age to settle—and rich as Croesus! If he seemed a trifle starchy to Sydney's taste, correct to a fault, she was quick to forgive this minor handicap in favor of the rancor in Lady Windham's breast. Aunt Harriet had been measuring the baron for Trixie, and now he was paying particular attention to Winifred. What more could Sydney ask?

Of course the regard of such a social prize brought its own complications. The baron took his position as seriously as Aunt Harriet took her purse. He would never go beyond the line, and his associates must also be beyond reproof. His bride would have to be pretty and prettily behaved, an ornament to Scoville's title. There could be no hint of straightened circumstances or hanging out for a fortune, no irregular behavior or questionable reputations, no running back to Little Dedham!

Sydney just had to get the money somewhere!

2

Rights and Responsibilities

If love were a loaf of bread, Forrest Mainwaring, Viscount Mayne, would resume his naval commission and eat sea biscuits for the rest of his life. He'd take the acres of his father's holdings under his management out of grains and he'd plant mangel-wurzels instead. Love was a bore and a pestilence that would choke the very life out of a man. If he let it.

"They'll never get us, eh, Nelson?" The viscount nudged his companion, a scruffy one-eyed hound. Nelson rolled over and went back to sleep at Lord Mayne's feet.

"You're no better than Spottswood," his lordship complained, thinking of the latest of his friends to turn benedict. Old Spotty used to be the best of good fellows, eager for a run down to Newmarket for the races or a night of cards. And now? Now Spotty was content to sit by the fire with his blushing bride. Mayne would blush, too, if he had so little conversation. Gads, Spotty was as dull as . . . a dog.

Then there was Haverstoke, another one-time friend. Six months he'd been leg-shackled. Six months, by Jupiter, and he was already afraid of turning his back on the lightskirt he'd wed lest she plant horns on his head. "She would, too," Forrest told the sleeping dog. "She's tried to catch me alone often enough."

Nigel Thompson had wed a Diamond. Now he was bankrupting his estate to keep the shrew in emeralds and ermine. The viscount poured himself another brandy and settled back in his worn leather chair. "Females . . ."

Just then a plaintive howl echoed through the night. Nelson's nose twitched. His ears quivered. Squire Beck's setter bitch! The old dog was through the library window before his master could complete the thought: "Bah."

Forrest was not quite the misogynist his father purported to be; the duke would expound on his pet theory at the drop of an aged cognac. Hamilton Mainwaring believed, so he said, that since women's bones were lighter, their bodies less well-muscled, and their skulls smaller, they couldn't possibly think as well as men. On the other hand, the Duke of Mayne would relate to his cronies at Whites, their brains were so stuffed with frills and furbelows, it was no wonder they made no sense. No one ever asked the duchess's opinion.

The viscount did not share his father's views, not entirely. He had great respect for his mother, Sondra, Duchess of Mayne. He even felt affection for his two flighty sisters, more so now that they were married and living at opposite ends of England. He also had a connoisseur's appreciation for womanhood in general, and several discrete widows, a few high-born ladies with lower instincts, and the occasional select demi-mondaine in particular. Forrest Mainwaring was not a monk. Neither was he a womanizer. At twenty-nine, he was considered by the ton to be worldly, and too wise to be caught in parson's mousetrap. The viscount was a true nonpareil, one of the most attractive men in town, with extensive understanding and accomplishments in the fields of business, agriculture, the arts, and athletics. In addition, he was wealthy in his own right. Lord Mayne would have made a prime prize on the marriage mart if his views on the subject were not so well known. Zeus, he thought without conceit, he'd be hunted down like a rabid dog if the grasping mamas thought he could be cornered.

He couldn't. The Duke of Mayne was in rude good health, and Forrest's younger brother, Brennan, provided a more than adequate heir. His sisters were busy filling their nurseries, so the succession was assured. Forrest saw no other reason for him to submit to the ties that bind.

Bind, hell, the viscount considered, taking another sip of his glass. Bind, choke, strangle, fetter, hobble, maim. He shook his head, disarranging the dark curls. He liked women well enough; it was marriage, or the double yoke of love and marriage, that had this decorated hero quaking in his Hessians.

The viscount did not need his friends' experiences to set him against the state of matrimony and the toils of love. He'd had enough examples aboard ship, when his fellow officers would discover their sweethearts had found someone else or, worse, their wives had. And the lovesick young ensigns, sighing like mooncalves over some heartless charmer, had

Lieutenant Mainwaring feeling all the symptoms of *mal de mer*. No, even those reminders came too late; he'd learned his lessons far earlier, at his parents' knees. His mother's in Sussex, his father's in London.

To say the Duke and Duchess of Mayne were estranged was gilding the lily. They were strange. They hardly spoke, seldom visited, and continued through years of separation to send each other tender greetings of affection—via their sons. And what a legendary love match theirs had been!

Hamilton and Sondra were neighbors, he the heir to a fortune and a trusted place at court, she the only child of a land-rich squire. They were too young, and from far different backgrounds and stations in life, so both sets of parents disapproved of the match. Naturally the young people eloped.

The early years proved them right. They were deliriously happy, spreading their time between travel on the Continent, joining the London swirl at the highest ranks, and riding for days over their lush fields, reveling in nature's bounty. Then Hamilton ascended to his father's dignities and, soon after, Sondra's father's acreage. Sondra started breeding, and the foundation of their marriage started cracking, along with every dish and piece of bric-a-brac in one castle, three mansions, and two hunting boxes.

Sondra wanted a nest; Hamilton wanted a foreign legation. The duchess loved the peace of the estates; the duke craved the excitement of court. She wanted a country squire; he wanted a political hostess. Mr. Spode had a standing order.

Children only aggravated the situation. Wet nurses versus mother's milk, home tutors versus boarding schools, pinafores for the boys, ponies for the girls—everything was a bone of contention, and more crockery would fly. Finally the duke did accept an ambassadorship.

"If you leave the country, I shall never speak to you again," Lady Mayne swore.

"Is that a promise?" Lord Mayne replied, already packing. "Well, if you don't come with me, I shall never speak to *you* again," he countered.

He went, she didn't, and they enclosed loving messages in their children's letters. The senior Lord Mayne returned often enough to toss a china shepherdess or two and drag his children into the tug-of-war. Forrest should be groomed for political life by running for a seat in the Commons, the duke decided. The duchess thought he should pursue further studies, as befitted a man with vast holdings to overlook, since his father neglected those duties. The young viscount bought himself a commission and ran away to sea. The French blockade was more peaceful than life between the Maynes. That was some years earlier, and now they were arguing, through the mails of course, about Brennan's future. At twenty-two Bren should have been making his own decisions, but his mother swore she would die of a broken heart if another son went off to war, and his father was holding out all the glitter of the City to keep the boy from turning into a country bumpkin.

So Mother raised dogs and roses in Sussex and the governor raised votes and issues in Parliament and the privy council. Brennan raised hell in London like every well-breeched young greenheaded sprig before him . . . and Forrest Mainwaring, Viscount Mayne, raised his glass.

It was his lot, though the Lord knew what he'd done to deserve the task, to look out for all of them. He moved between estates and far-flung holdings in the country, banking institutions and bawdy houses in the city, trying to safeguard the family investments and Brennan's family jewels. He managed Mayne Chance, the ducal seat, and struggled to keep staff on at Mainwaring House in Grosvenor Square. The turnover in servants was not surprising considering the duke's penchant for tossing the tableware; it was just difficult for his son.

Life in the country was not noticeably easier. Mother filled the castle with dogs: tiny, tawny, repulsive Pekingese, with their curling tongues, pop eyes, and shrill yips. Lady Mayne said raising the creatures was more satisfying than raising children. A man could not walk without fear of tripping over one of the ugly little blighters nor sit down without finding that gingery hair all over his superfines. Worse, a man could not even bring his own pet, his own (sometimes) loyal dog, Nelson, into the house. On the hound's last, unsanctioned visit, Nelson had caught one glimpse of the little rodents in fur coats and, knowing that no real dog was fluffed and perfumed and beribboned, he did his level one-eyed best to rid Mayne Chance of such vermin. Banished, he was, and his master with him.

Viscount Mayne sat alone and lonely amongst the holland covers in the dower house library, still cold despite the new-laid fire. His hair was mussed, his broad shoulders were bent with the weight of the world—and the Mainwarings—on them, and he'd have a devilish headache in the morning. He should have stayed in the navy, Forrest thought as he contemplated the most recent missives from his loving parents.

My dearest son, his mother wrote from ten minutes away, *How I miss you.* The viscount almost laughed. She'd most likely have moved Princess Pennyfeather and the bitch's latest litter into his bedroom by now. Forrest skimmed over the body of the letter—gads, he'd been gone only a day and a half. Whipslade's prize bull Fred got into Widow Lang's garden again, a tile was loose on the south wing, Reverend Jamison thought the tower bell might have a crack in it, and the Albertsons were coming to dinner tomorrow. The viscount would see to the first three in the morning, and see that he was otherwise engaged by the evening. Lady Mayne wanted grandsons or revenge, Forrest never knew which. The Albertsons had a daughter.

I am worried about your brother, the letter continued in the duchess's delicate copperplate. Not Brennan, but your brother. That meant trouble. Lady Mayne had a network of information gatherers spread through the ton which would put Napoleon's secret police to shame. Bren's larks usually flew home in the next post, where the duchess could cheerfully shred his character to bits and lay the pieces at his father's door. Of course the duke was to blame for *his* son's peccadillos; the boy was always properly behaved in the country. When Brennan became Forrest's brother, she wanted the viscount to handle the bumblebroth. Dash it, Lord Mayne cursed, he wasn't the lad's keeper. He didn't have time to rush off to London to tear the cawker out of some doxie's talons, no matter how homely the Albertsons' daughter was. For once, though, there was no mention of a female anywhere in his mother's enumeration of Brennan's misdeeds and character flaws, not even between the lines. Usually she would refer to "persons about whose existence a lady is supposed to have no knowledge." This epistle was filled with basket scramblers, gallows bait, and ivory tuners instead. Those were some of the fonder epithets she was tossing at her youngest child's head. No, the viscount realized when he reread the rambling paragraph, sure he'd find a Paphian in there somewhere; the basket scramblers, gallows bait, et al., were the villains of the piece. Brennan, for once, was an innocent lamb being led to the slaughter through his father's neglect. Someone, she wrote, would have to save her baby from the wolves.

"She must mean you, old fellow," the viscount told Nelson when the hound vaulted back in through the window, leaving muddy footprints on the carpet. " 'Cause I ain't going."

When you get to London, Her Grace concluded, not if, but when, *give your dear father my fondest regards and tell him I wish he were here by my side.*

The viscount shook his head and scratched behind the hound's ears. Nelson drooled on his master's boots, radiating affection and the mixed aroma of swamp and stable. Now there was a man's dog.

The duke's writing was firm and bold; his letter was short and succinct, the antithesis of his lady wife's style, naturally. *Forrest, Your brother*—they seemed to have something in common, after all—*is in a spot of trouble, but do not let the duchess hear of it lest she worry. The doctor says he'll be fine. You might suggest your mother come to London for the beginning of the Season. Tell her I miss the waltzes we used to share. P.S. We need a new butler.*

"Dash it, Father, why couldn't you have thrown the inkwell at your new secretary instead of at Potts? Educated young fellows are as common as fleas on a dog, but a good butler . . ."

The duke was looking hopefully out to the carriage, where a footman was carrying in Forrest's bags. The light seemed to go out of his eyes when the coach proved empty.

"She did send you her best wishes," the viscount hurried on, "and some apples from the west orchard. She remembered they were your favorites, Your Grace."

"What's that? Oh, yes, apples. No, I must get back to Whitehall straightaway. Did I tell you we might get passage of the Madden-Oates Bill finally?" A second footman stood ready to hand the duke his hat and cane.

"But what about Brennan?"

"No, I don't think he'd like any apples either. Loose teeth, don't you know."

His Grace departed and Forrest temporarily promoted the sturdiest-looking footman. Then he went upstairs.

Forrest almost did not recognize the man in the bed. The viscount was even more alarmed when he considered that Brennan was usually his own mirror image, less a few years and worry lines. Like peas in a pod, they shared the same dark curls and square jaw, the same clear blue eyes and the authoritative Mainwaring nose. They used to anyway.

His lordship's next thought, after vowing mayhem to whoever had done this to his brother, was to thank the heavens the duchess hadn't come to London after all. If the idea of Bren's putting on a uniform sent Lady Mayne into spasms, he could not imagine her reaction to the sorry specimen between the sheets.

"What in bloody hell happened to you, you gossoon?"

Bren opened one eye, the one not swollen closed and discolored. He tried to smile without moving his jaw, winced, and gave up on the effort. He raised one linen-swathed hand in greeting. "The governor send for you?" he asked.

"No, His Grace merely needed a new butler."

Bren sighed. "I suppose it was Mother who sent in the big guns."

"It was either London or the brig on hardtack and bilge water." Forrest dragged a chair closer to the bed and carefully pulled the covers over his brother's bandaged chest.

"I can handle it," Bren said, looking away.

"I can see that."

The younger man flushed, not an attractive addition to the yellow and purple blotches. He cleared his throat and Forrest held a glass to his cut lip so he could drink. "Thank you. Ah, how is Mother?"

"In alt. Princess Pennyfeather had four pups, all that coppery color she's been after. Of course I wasn't permitted to see the new additions. I might disturb the princess, don't you know."

"She's daft when it comes to those dogs, ain't she?"

"My dear Brennan, anyone else would have been committed to Bedlam long since. Mother is a duch-

23

ess, however, so she is merely eccentric." Forrest picked a speck of lint off his fawn breeches. Then he inspected his Hessians for travel dust.

"You ain't going to be happy."

"I'm already overjoyed, bantling."

"I didn't ask you to get involved."

Viscount Mayne stood to his full six foot height, his legs spread and his arms crossed over his chest. Men had been known to tremble before Lieutenant Mainwaring in his quarterdeck command. "Cut line, mister. I am here and I am not leaving. I'd go after anyone who treated a dog this way. Perhaps not one of Mother's rug rats, but my own brother? They must have loosened a few spokes in your wheel if you think I'll just walk away. No one, I repeat, no one, harms one of mine."

"Well, there was this woman . . ."

"I knew it!"

3

Might and Mayne

The woman was not to blame. Not that a pretty little redheaded opera dancer wouldn't have taken Brennan's money and laid him low; she just hadn't—yet.

"They were giving a benefit performance after the regular show that night, so I had a lot of hours to kill before I could meet Mademoiselle Rochelle."

"A French *artiste. Je comprende.*"

"I'm not such a green 'un as all that. Roxy's no more French than I am. She's not even much of a dancer, and I found out straightaway she sure as hell ain't a natural redhead. Still . . ." He shrugged, as much as two strapped ribs would allow.

"Still, you had a lot of hours to kill."

"So I had a few drinks with Tolly before he went on to Lady Bessborough's. He needed it; she's his godmother and has her niece in mind for him. So I toddled off to White's."

"And had a few drinks there."

"Dash it, Forrest, that ain't the point. I can hold my liquor."

The viscount studied his manicure. His brother swallowed hard before going on. "White's was as quiet as a tomb. You know, the governor's cronies nodding over their newspapers. I decided to step over to the Cocoa Tree. Don't raise your eyebrow at me, I know the play gets too deep for my pockets there. I just had a glass or two of Daffy and watched Martindale lose his watch fob, his diamond stick pin, and his new curricle and pair to Delverson."

"Dare I hope it was an illuminating experience?"

"What's that? Oh, d'you mean did I learn anything? Sure. I'll never game against Delverson. Fellow's got the devil's own luck. Anyway," he continued over his brother's sigh of exasperation, "Martindale knew of a place where the stakes weren't so high and drinks were free. Since I still had a few hours before I could go back to the theater, I went along. I know what you're going to say. I ought to, by George, you've said it often enough: Don't play where you don't know the table. But the place looked respectable enough—not first stare, don't you know—and I recognized some of the fellows at the tables. The long and the short of it is, we sat down to play."

"And had a few drinks?"

"And had a few drinks. They were serving Blue Ruin. I think now that it may have been tampered with."

"Undoubtedly, but do go on, Bren, you're finally beginning to get interesting. Or wise."

"You ain't making this any easier, you know. Anyway, the stakes weren't real high, and I wasn't laying out much of the ready, 'cause I needed it for later and, ah, Roxy. Martindale lost his ring and decided his luck was out, so he quit and went home. I should have left with him."

"But you still had a few hours to fill."

"And credit in the bank, with the quarter nearly over and next quarter's allowance due. So I stayed, won a little, lost a little. Fellow by the name of Chester was holding the bank. Otto Chester. He seemed a gentleman. You know, clean hands, clean linen. Wouldn't have seemed out of place at White's. I signed over a couple of vouchers to him, nothing big, mind, and then I went home."

The viscount was up and pacing, having reached the ends of even his copious patience. "What do you mean, then you went home? Then you were set on by a pack of footpads? Then you were mowed down by a runaway carriage?"

"Then I went home. My head was too heavy for my neck and my eyes didn't fit in their sockets. My insides felt like I'd swallowed a live eel. I didn't think I was so castaway; I just thought it must have been from mixing my drinks all night. Anyway, I wasn't going to be much good to Roxy, and I was afraid I'd embarrass myself by casting up accounts on her shoes or something, so I sent her a note and took a hackney home."

Forrest ran his fingers through his hair, wondering whether he'd pull it all out or turn gray before this tale was told. He frowned at his brother and told him, "You know, you take after Mother."

"And when you knot your eyebrows together like that and start shouting, you remind me of the governor. Just don't throw anything 'cause I can't duck right now. There's not much more to tell anyway.

"The next morning I woke up late, stopped by the

27

bank to withdraw the balance, and at Rundell's to pick out a trinket for Roxy. Then I called on Mr. Chester at the address on his card, to redeem my vowels. Only he didn't have them. Said he had expenses of his own, gambling losses he had to meet, so he'd sold *my* notes to a moneylender to get money to pay off *his* debts. Have you ever heard the like? A gentleman would have given a chap to the end of the week, at least. Well, I told him what I thought of such a scurvy move, in no uncertain terms, you can be sure."

"I bet you threatened to call him out."

Brennan smiled, and a tiny glimmer of the blue spark showed in his one good eye. "Worse. I swore never to play with him again. At any rate, I went to the new address, somebody Randall, an Irish Shylock. I introduce myself, tell him I want to settle up—and damned if this Randall says I don't owe hundreds, I owe thousands! With interest building every day. He shows me chits that look like my hand, but they couldn't be. I don't have that kind of blunt and I didn't play that deep, I swear."

"I believe you, cawker," Forrest said. He rested his hand on his brother's shoulder. "So what happened? You went after Randall?"

Brennan cursed in disgust. "I didn't even get the chance. He whistles and this ogre as big as a house lurches out of a side room. Next thing I know, I'm lying in the gutter. They've got my purse, my watch, and Roxy's bracelet. Goliath is grinning and the bastard Irishman is claiming I still owe a thousand pounds. Says he'll go to the governor if I don't pay up in a week, or send his bully to call to remind me." He winced. "As if I could forget."

"You can. Just rest now, I'll take care of it."

All of it. The bogus debt, the bone crusher, the bloodsucker, and the cardsharp.

Forrest Mainwaring really was an even-tempered, mild-mannered gentleman to the dignified core. He was tolerant, temperate, thoughtful, and slow to anger. He waited till after luncheon.

First he sent a note to his mother, assuring her of Brennan's welfare and, out of habit, his father's continuing devotion. Then he checked some of the accounts, sent a note round to a new hiring agency, and made an excellent meal of turbot in oyster sauce, veal Marsala, a taste of rarebit, tomatoes in aspic, and cherry trifle.

Viscount Mayne proceeded methodically down his list. His first stop was the bank, his second Rundell and Bridges, the jewelers. After consulting their sales records, the store's manager was able to find a duplicate of Mademoiselle Rochelle's erstwhile gift. Forrest matched the simple bracelet to a necklace set with emeralds—a redhead, *n'est-ce pas?*—and dangling earbobs.

"Coo-ee," Bren's *chérie* exclaimed in perfect cockney. "If those ain't the dabbest sparklers Oi ever seen!" Having seen a bit of the world herself, she knew the meaning of such a generous gift. " 'E's not comin' back, then, your love of a brother?"

"His illness is more than a trifling indisposition, he regrets. He did not want you to wait."

"Ain't that a real gentleman." She was admiring the effect of her new possessions in a smoky glass over a dressing table littered with bottles and jars and powders. She suddenly spun around to face His

Lordship, eyes wide with concern. " 'Tain't nothin' catchy-like, is it?"

Forrest's lips curved in a slow smile. "Nothing he won't outgrow."

"That's all right, then." Roxy considered that smile, and the viscount's well-muscled figure leaning nonchalantly against the door frame. "Oi don't suppose you'd . . . ?"

Lord Mayne's head shook, but his smile widened, showing even white teeth.

Roxy turned back to her reflection. "Well, you can't blame a girl for tryin'."

"*Au contraire, chérie*, I am honored." He raised her hands to his lips in farewell. "*Enchanté, mademoiselle.*"

"Enchant-tea to you too, ducky."

The proprietor of the gaming rooms on King Street recognized the crest on the carriage. It was Alf Sniddon's business to know such things. He made sure his doorman told Viscount Mayne the place was closed till evening. The doorman made sure he'd stay alive till evening instead, and was therefore richer by a handsome tip besides. The place was open for business, but not for long, it seemed, unless Mr. Sniddon changed his policy.

"But I don't make the bets or take the young gentlemen's vouchers, my lord."

"No, you take only a hefty cut of the winnings. Let me put it this way, Sniddon: How long would you stay in business if word went out in the clubs that you ran a crooked table, plucking young pigeons with drugged wine?"

Sniddon calculated how long it would take to find new quarters, change the name of the establishment, change *his* name, establish a new clientele. It was cheaper to change policies.

"Right-o, cash on the barrel it is, my lord, for all young gentlemen."

"There, I knew we could agree. And who knows, you might just set a new style, an honest gaming hell. I'd be tempted to stop in myself."

Sniddon recognized Mayne's soft-spoken words for the mixed blessing they were: a threat that the powerful lord would be monitoring Sniddon's compliance, and a promise of reward, for where the handsome viscount led, his well-heeled Corinthian set followed. Sniddon nodded. He'd try it the nob's way a while, then move if he had to. It wouldn't be the first time.

So much for business. The viscount tapped his cane on the coach roof to signal his driver on to the next destination. It was time for pleasure.

Otto Chester lived in rooms at 13 Jermyn Street, where accommodations were cheap because of foolish superstitions. Such imbecilic notions meant little to a man used to making his own luck with marked decks and loaded dice. Today his luck was out. Otto Chester wished he'd been out, too. Instead, he was in the act of setting the folds in his neckcloth when Lord Forrest Mainwaring strode into the room without waiting to be announced. Fate seldom makes an appointment.

Chester was a jackal dressed in gentlemen's togs. He was everything Viscount Mayne despised: pale, weak, preying on the unwary like a back-biting cur. In short, he was a coward, not even attempting to regain his feet after Forrest's first hard right.

"But—" he gulped around the rock-hard fist that was embedded in the material of his neckcloth, dragging him up and holding his feet off the ground. He batted ineffectively at the viscount's steely right arm with an effete left. "But I had notes of my own. You know, debts of honor, play and pay."

Forrest sneered in disgust. There wasn't any satisfaction in darkening the dirty dealer's daylights; the paltry fellow was already quaking in his boots. On second thought, he reflected, there might be a modicum of satisfaction in cramming the muckworm's mockery of the gentleman's credo down his scrawny throat. "You wouldn't recognize honor if it hit you on the nose," he growled, following through with a cross punch to said protuberance. "Now you will."

Lord Mayne tossed the offal aside like a pile of rags and wiped his hands on a fresh neckcloth waiting in reserve on a nearby chair back. He threw it to the sniveling scum in the corner. "Here, fix yourself up. We're going for a ride."

4

Debt and Dishonor

$\mathcal{T}$he office of O. Randall and Associates, Financial Consultants, was located on Fleet Street in convenient view of the debtors' prison. Randall himself was a small, stocky man a few years older than Forrest, he guessed, with carroty hair, a soft Irish brogue, and hard, calculating eyes. Those eyes shifted from his distinguished caller sitting at ease across the desk to the sorry lumpkin huddled in an uncomfortable wooden chair in the shadows. As far away from his lordship as the room would allow, Chester dabbed an already-crimson neckcloth to his broken nose. Randall's gaze quickly left the gory sight and returned to the viscount.

"And may I pour ye a bit of Ireland's best, me lord?" he offered. "No? Well, 'tis a wise man who knows his limits. That's what I tried to tell the lad, I did. A fine boy, young Mainwaring, an' the spit an' image of yourself, b'gorn. 'Twas sorry I was to see him in a mite of trouble."

"We were all sorry. That's why I am here."

Randall poured himself a drink. "Ah, family feeling. 'Tis a fine thing indeed." He shot a dark look toward Chester's corner. "Never had a brother o' me heart m'self. Never regretted it more than today."

For all his relaxed manner, Lord Mayne had no desire to discuss his family with any loan shark. He reached to his inside pocket and retrieved a leather purse. Tossing it to the desk with a satisfying thud and the jangle of heavy coins, he announced, "There's your thousand pounds. You can count it if you wish, but the Mainwarings always pay their debts. *Always*."

Randall missed the danger in the viscount's silky "always," too busy scheming. His eyes on the sack, he sipped his drink and licked his thick lips. "Well now, a thousand pounds was the figure two days ago. Ye do ken the nature o' me business, would ye now?"

Slowly, with careful deliberation, Forrest removed his pigskin gloves while he addressed the third man in the room. "What do you think, Mr. Chester?"

Chester clutched the stained cravat to his nose as if to hold all his remaining courage inside. Wild-eyed over the cloth, he babbled, "I fink a fousand pounds is fine."

Lord Mayne smiled. Randall didn't like the smile, and the leather purse *had* played his favorite tune. He nodded and reached out for the gold. The viscount's iron grip was around his wrist before Randall could say *compound interest*. "The chits?"

"For sure an' we're all bein' reasonable men conductin' a little business." Randall pulled a chain with a ring of keys out of his pocket, selected one, and opened the top drawer of his desk. Then he used another key to open a side drawer. Glancing quickly back and forth between Forrest and the pouch, he withdrew a stack of papers. He slid them across to the viscount, keeping one hand close to the open top drawer.

Forrest checked the signatures. They were a good enough forgery to pass for Brennan's. He nudged the leather purse toward the Irishman, who put both hands on the desk to draw it closer.

The viscount proceeded to rip up the vouchers. When that chore was finished to his satisfaction, with small, narrow pieces, he started to move around the desk, prepared to rip up the Irishman.

There was that smile again, and a glimmer of anticipation in Mayne's blue eyes. The moneylender finally realized he'd been petting a panther instead of a lapcat. He pursed his lips to whistle but, instead of a breath of air, he suddenly found a fist in his mouth.

It was hard to whistle with a mouthful of blood, so Randall went for the gun in the top drawer. That was an error. The viscount dove headfirst across the desk, reaching for the weapon. He flung Randall's arm up at the height of his lunge, then crashed to the ground with Randall under him. The pistol discharged its one ball, wounding the ceiling grievously, sending plaster down on all of them.

Forrest stood up, brushing at the white dust in his hair. Randall managed to get to his knees, where he tried to whistle again. This proved an impossibility with his two front teeth gone missing. So he reached down for the knife in his boot.

The viscount was grinning. "Thanks for evening the odds. I hate to maul a smaller man. It's not gentlemanly, but you wouldn't know about that, would you?" He removed his coat and wrapped it about his left arm, all the while keeping an eye on the little man.

Now, Lord Mayne had his superb physical condition from working alongside his laborers in the country, and his boxing science from sparring with Gentleman Jackson himself whenever he was in town, but he had his gutter instincts from his naval days. Dark quays and stench-ridden harbors were excellent school yards for dirty fighting, where there was nothing to keep a pack a cutthroats from your wallet but your fists and your wits. In the dark you didn't wait to see if your opponent was giving you fair odds. He never was.

Randall was shouting, "Whithtle, Chethter, whithtle," as he lost his knife to a well-placed kick. Then he lost the use of his hand to a vicious chop. Then he lost his lunch to a fist in the breadbasket.

Between Randall's retches and moans, Chester asked "Wha?"

Forrest wasn't even breathing hard. He looked at the man, still in his corner, still nursing his broken nose. "He means 'whistle.' "

"Whiddle?"

"Yes, man, whistle. Go on, do it."

If Forrest had said "fly," Chester would likely have tried flapping his arms. He puckered his lips and tweeted—the opening bars of *la Marseillaise*!

Forrest shook his head. "Spineless and a traitor to boot. Here, man, let me do it." He put two fingers in his mouth and let loose a piercing shrill that almost always brought Nelson to heel.

Sam Odum was as big as Brennan had said, and twice as ugly. Bald, scarred, and snaggle-toothed, he lumbered into the room swinging a piece of kindling. Odum's kindling was more like a medium-size tree, but who was going to quibble with him about starting a fire? The ape paused in the middle of the room, looking around in confusion.

"Your employer is on the floor behind the desk," Forrest pointed out helpfully. "We've had a small disagreement. The gentleman with the interesting headpiece"—nodding in Chester's direction—"has wisely selected a neutral corner. Have you any opinions on the matter?"

Sam Odum scratched his head, then his crotch. "Huh?"

Randall spat out, "Kill him," along with another tooth, so Sam Odum hefted his club and plodded in Chester's direction.

"Not him, you ath! The thwell!"

Sam Odum was confused again, not an unusual occurrence, it seemed. Gentleman that he was, Mainwaring decided to help the poor bastard identify his intended victim. He tossed a chair at him. It missed, but the hard right that followed didn't. Sam staggered, but came back swinging the bat. Forrest was ready with the other chair. He used it as a shield to parry a blow that could have decapitated him, then followed by smashing the chair over the mammoth's head. The chair broke, and Sam Odum just staggered a little more. And kept swinging that blasted tree trunk. Forrest kept ducking, getting in punches where he could, getting battered when he couldn't.

There were no more chairs except the one Chester crouched behind. Forrest backed toward the desk and swept the papers, all those little shreds, into Odum's ugly phiz. While the ogre was distracted, the viscount finally managed to land a kick and a punch and a jab and another punch. Odum still stood, but at least the club had come dislodged from his hamlike fist. Now Forrest could close in for some real boxing.

No human could stand that kind of punishment. Sam Odum wasn't human. "Oh, hell," Lord Mayne swore, then took the small pistol from his boot. He turned it around and whacked the bruiser alongside the head.

That brought him to his knees. Forrest threw all his remaining strength into a blow to Odum's chin, then grabbed him by both ears and banged his head into the floor.

"Now that I have your attention"—wham!—"this is for my brother." Wham. "And this"—wham!—"is for kicking him while he was down." There was now a considerable dent in the floor, to say nothing of Sam Odum's head. He stayed put when Forrest took his hands away.

The viscount looked around to see if anyone else was offering further entertainment. Randall was still moaning and Chester appeared to be praying. Forrest pocketed the pistol and Randall's knife, out of temptation's way. He didn't think he'd be tempted to skewer either of the muckworms, but one never knew. He hauled the unconscious bully to the doorway and shoved him down the outside stairs.

"Take him to the docks," he ordered his driver and waiting footmen, "and find the recruiting officer. Give my name and tell him I said Mr. Sam Odum is dying to join the navy."

"Well, gentlemen, now that I've introduced myself, shall we discuss *my* terms?"

The question was entirely rhetorical; Chester and Randall sat bound and gagged on the floor in front of the desk. On Forrest's return from disposing of the late debt-collector, he'd found Randall creeping toward Sam Odum's tiny "office" and the small arsenal stashed there. "How convenient," the viscount murmured, gently tapping the Irishman's fingers with a length of lead pipe. He swept all but two pieces of rope into a carpetbag nearby for later removal. The two associates wouldn't be needing weapons. He tied Randall for safety's sake, "So you don't hurt yourself during our little talk," and stuffed the man's neckcloth in his mouth to stop his foul curses. He did the same to the taller man, whose whining pleas were embarrassing both of them, then took his seat in what was left of Randall's chair.

"Where were we? Oh, yes, terms. You can keep the thousand pounds—it was worth every shilling—and your lives. Of course, that's assuming I never see either of you again or hear my family name mentioned in connection with you or your filth.

"As for you," he said, fixing Otto Chester in his blue-dagger gaze. Chester cringed back as far as his bonds would permit. "You are finished in London. You'll never be admitted to the better clubs for being a Captain Sharp, and word will be sent to even the lowest dives that you're not particularly good at it. I should think that if I passed on my doubts as to your loyalty to the Crown, to say nothing of your manhood, you'd have a hard enough time in this city finding flats to gull. You might do better on the Continent. Am I understood?"

Chester nodded vigorously, which disturbed a small cloud of plaster dust that had fallen from the ceiling into his hair. He looked like one of the tiny snowmen in a crystal dome, a child's plaything.

There was nothing so innocuous about O. Randall. Venom flowed from him in near-tangible waves.

"I could bring charges against you, you know," the viscount told him. "Usury, extortion, forgery, paying someone to assault a nobleman, threatening violence to a peer of the realm. I could make the charges stick, even if Uncle Donald weren't Lord High Magistrate. But trash like you isn't worth my time or effort. I'd prefer you to slink off to find some other rock to hide behind. Let us just see how many others would miss you if you go."

He started to go through the drawers, tossing another pistol and a wicked stiletto into the carpetbag near his side of the desk. His eye caught on a tray of calling cards.

"Otto Randall," he read aloud. "How curious, considering the only other Otto I knew was a Prussian, and now there are two in the same room and almost the same profession." Forrest looked from Otto Randall to Otto Chester and shrugged, returning to the drawers. When he reached the files with the moneylender's receipts, he began separating the chits into three piles. One stack was for men who could afford to play deep, or those so bitten by the gambling fever they would only find another source of money to support their habit. One fairly notorious courtesan had a folder of her own. No wonder she'd been sending billets-doux to half the well-heeled coves in town. Let her pay Randall back in trade, he decided grimly; that would be enough of a lesson. The second stack was of names unknown to the viscount, or men whose circumstances were not broadcast in the clubs. Half of these he ripped into shreds, calling it the luck of the draw. The other half he added to the first pile. The third and largest collection of chits belonged to young men like his brother, young scholars and country squires without town bronze to protect them, or other innocents up River Tick. He frowned over four slips with one name, a friend who should have known better. Then again, Manfrey's wife was a virago; it was no wonder he stayed out late gambling. Lord Mayne added two of Manfrey's vouchers to the first pile and added the other two to the third stack. These he tucked into a pocket of his coat, now draped across the back of his chair.

"Consider this batch of debts canceled. I'll see to them." He straightened the remaining papers and nodded toward Randall. "This is your share. You ought to be able to settle up with these loose screws in a week. After that you are out of business and out of town. There will be a warrant for your arrest and one very conscientious citizen to see that the warrant is served. You don't want that, do you?"

Before Randall could give answer, grunt, nod, or whatever choice was open to him, a knock sounded on the door. Forrest cursed softly and waited to hear the footsteps recede down the outer stairs. He did not want to be bothered with someone creating a public scene or calling the watch; he still had to interview butlers that afternoon.

He quickly dragged both Ottos into Sam Odum's cubby and shoved them to the rank palette on the floor. "And Father thought politics made strange bedfellows," he mused as the tall, pale Englishman sank thankfully into the ticking while the banty, red-faced Irishman still struggled against his ropes. Forrest was trying to close the door around their jutting legs when the knock was repeated with more force.

"Damn. Some poor bastard can't wait to sell his soul to these two bankers from hell."

5

Hair and There

Cravats were handy items with myriad uses: bandages, gags, nose wipes, napkins, white flags of surrender. And a decorative essential to a gentleman's haberdashery. Forrest's once precision-folded Oriental was now a limp, mangled, blood-spattered bit of evidence to recent events. He removed it on his way to the door and dabbed at a cut on his lip. He could only hope the bruise on his jaw, where Odum's club had connected, was not already discolored. At least no one could tell that his ribs were aching.

He opened the outer door and looked up, and up, then silently groaned. No one else might know, but Forrest's body was telling him it was in no condition to handle another belligerent behemoth. And this blond fellow in the doorway was big, way taller than the viscount's own six feet, and broad. And solidly built. And young. If he was in Randall's employ . . . It was too late to run like hell, so Forrest did the next best thing. He smiled.

The caller hesitated, still uncertain of what *he* confronted, then nodded. "My employer," he said, indicating a waiting hackney, "requests an interview with Mr. Otto Randall." He held out a calling card with the corner turned down to show the visitor had come in person.

Forrest belatedly noted the man's neat livery uniform, a footman of some sort, then, and glanced quickly at the card. He didn't recognize the name *Sydney Lattimore*, in fancy script, but he could guess the type. He'd be a nervous, effeminate man-milliner, judging by the curlicues surrounding his name, afraid to venture into a den of iniquity by himself, hence the sturdy bodyguard. He was no man-about-town—Mayne would have made his acquaintance otherwise—nor was he among the other debtors in Randall's file. Forrest surmised he was a young sprig who'd tipped the dibs and punted on tick. The least Forrest could do for the muttonhead was play Good Samaritan with some good advice.

"Tell your employer that he doesn't want anything to do with moneylenders. He should stay out of gaming parlors if he can't make the ante, and away from his tailor if he can't pay the shot, if that's his weakness. Tell him that his pride can stand a bout with honest employment better than it can a sentence in the Fleet, which is where he'll end up, dealing with the sharks."

The footman nodded sagely, tugged at the tight collar of his uniform, and started back down the stairs. Halfway toward the waiting carriage he remembered he had a job to do. "But, Mr. Randall, sir . . ."

Gads, that anyone would think he was one of the Ottos! That's what came of playing at guardian angel. Damnation, what kind of angel had his shirt half torn and his knuckles scraped and plaster dust trickling down his neck? Angry, Forrest shouted loudly enough to be heard from the carriage: "This establishment is closed, shut down, out of business. Thank your lucky stars and stay away from the bloodsuckers before you get bled dry."

He slammed the door and went back to get his coat and the satchel.

"Damn." He couldn't get his deuced coat on without skewing his ribs—and there was another blasted knock on the door. This benighted place saw as much traffic as Harriet Wilson's! He threw the door open.

"Double damn." Just what he needed, a woman. He looked down at the card he still held and noted what he'd missed the first time. *Miss* Sydney Lattimore. "Bloody hell." And a lady, judging by the shocked gasp from behind the black veil, the volume of concealing black swathes and shrouds, and the imperious way she brushed past him as if he were an upper servant, despite her small stature. She motioned the blond footman to wait outside. Now Forrest's day was complete: a little old spinster lady in mourning—she had enough crepe about her to mourn the entire British losses at Trafalgar—and her lapdog. She walked with teetery, unsure steps and kept trembly, black-gloved hands wrapped round the handle of a basket containing a miserable midget mutt. By Jupiter, Forrest would recognize that brassy Pekingese color in one of his nightmares. Fiend seize it, this *was* one of his nightmares. A friend of his mother's! The viscount could only wish Sam Odum back from the briny.

"No, ma'am," he began. "No, no, and no, whatever it is you want. The establishment is closed, the association disbanded. The Ottos are leaving town." He couldn't see behind the veil, but the old bat wasn't moving. "If you've swallowed a spider, go pop your ice."

A thin voice came to him weakly through the black drapery. "Spider? Ice?"

Of course she didn't understand cant. How could she, when the hag most likely hadn't been out of the house in ten years? Twenty, from the smell of mothballs about her withered, shrunken person. Lord Mayne took a deep breath, which his battered ribs protested, and started again. It just was not in his makeup to be rude to little old ladies. He'd likely be wasting his time with a rational explanation, but he had to try.

"Madam, if you have outrun the bailiff, you know, spent more than your pin money, I strongly urge you to retrench until your allowance comes due. Throw yourself on your relatives' mercy or confess to your trustees. You could pawn your valuables if you haven't already. Anything is preferable to dealing with the cents-per-centers. This office in particular is pulling in its shingle, and the profession in general is no fit association for a lady. It's a nasty, lowlife business, and borrowing will only bring you more grief than the money is worth. Please, please, ma'am, go home."

There, he'd tried. The little lady did not reply. Lord Mayne shrugged, turned to retrieve his coat and finally get out of there.

Sydney's jaws were glued shut in fear. Her legs were cemented to the floor with terror, but her knees wouldn't support her weight even if she did convince her feet to move. Dear heaven, what had she gotten herself into? This was even worse than her imaginings, which had been bad enough. She had spent a week getting her courage to the sticking point to approach this place, without her thinking she might have to face a half-naked savage shouting rough or incomprehensible language, a sack full of guns and knives, blood everywhere. Now she did not think she had enough courage left to make it down the stairs. On the other, shaking hand was *two* weeks of persuading herself that visiting a moneylender was her only choice. It still was. Sydney was determined to make the general proud. If he did not take another fit at what she was doing.

She swallowed—that was a start—and through sheer determination forced words past her dry lips. In a pitiful little voice she herself hardly recognized, Sydney asked, "Please, sir, could you tell me where else to go?"

She could go to Hades for all he cared! Botheration, hadn't the woman listened to a word he'd said? He dragged a hand through his hair in exasperation. "Miss L—" He remembered that the door to the anteroom was not quite shut. "Miss, I am trying to help you. Go home."

Sydney was fascinated by the white particles sifting from his hair, wondering what bizarre activities were conducted in these chambers. At least the humanizing gesture served to reassure her that the ruffian did not mean her bodily harm. She touched the basket's contents as if for confidence and, in tones more like her own, she informed him, "My need is great, sir, so I would appreciate the direction of one of your colleagues. In the ordinary course of events I wouldn't think of asking you to divulge a competitor, as it were, but since you seem reluctant to pursue your trade and my business is pressing . . ."

Reluctant? He was growing less and less reluctant about shoving the old hen down the stairs. If the witch wasn't already a friend of his mother's, she should be. They'd get along like cats and cream with that certainty of getting their own way and the mule-stubborn refusal to listen to logic.

". . . And I had a hard enough time getting your name and address."

"And how did you get, ah, my direction, if I might ask?" The viscount was stalling for time and inspiration, wondering if his conscience would permit him to make his escape and leave her with Chester and Randall. No, they'd had a bad enough day.

Sydney *really* wished he would offer her a seat before her knees gave way altogether, but she answered with still more assurance. "My abigail's former employer was Lady Motthaven. Her husband was a trifle behindtimes, and he borrowed to settle his debts. My maid recalled where he went for the loan."

"And did the abigail report that Motthaven repaid the loan easily?" The viscount knew he hadn't; the chit was on the desk. His words were measured, as if to a child.

Sydney looked down, shifted the basket from hand to hand. "They fled to the Continent. That's why the maid needed a new position."

"And did you not consider how Lord Motthaven's experience might relate to your own situation?" Hardened seamen would have sunk through the fo'castle deck at those silky tones. Sydney's chin came up.

"Yes, sir, I considered myself fortunate to acquire the services of an experienced lady's maid."

Sydney could not like the expression on Mr. Randall's face. He might have been an uncommonly attractive man but for the disfiguring bruises and the unfortunate continual scowl. Right now his eyes were narrowed and his mouth was pursed and Sydney thought she'd be more comfortable back in her carriage after all.

"Well, sir, I shall be going, then, seeing that you are determined to be unaccommodating. Far be it from me to tell you how to conduct your business, but I should wonder at your making a living at all, turning customers away." The moneylender growled. Yes, Sydney was sure that sound came from him. She edged closer to the door. Then she recalled her desperate need and the basket in her hand. She held it out. "Do you think, that is, if you could . . . ?"

Take her dog in pawn? The female must be queer in the attics for sure! The viscount backed away lest she put the plaguey thing in his hands. Only the desk kept him from backing through the wall.

"If you won't direct me to another moneylender, could you help me find someone who buys hair?"

"Hair? The dog is your hair? I mean, you have your hair in the basket?" Lord Mayne knew he was blathering. He couldn't help himself. That glorious red-gold shade, that sun-kissed honey fire, was her hair? He collapsed unawares into the chair. Brassy Pekingese? What addlepate thought that?

Sydney took the chair opposite, ignoring its missing arm and her host's lack of courtesy in not offering her a seat. One had to make allowances for the lower orders. After all, one should not expect polished manners from a usurer, nor from a madman for that matter. So far Sydney could not decide which he was, hostile barbarian or befuddled lackwit, sitting there now with his mouth hanging open. At least he seemed more disposed to assist her. Subtly, she thought, she used her foot to nudge the bag of weapons closer to her side of the desk, then started to lift her veil. "May I?" she asked.

"Oh, please do." The viscount gave himself a mental shake to recall his surroundings. "That is, suit yourself." Still, he held his breath. That gorgeous, vibrant mane could not belong to a shriveled old hag. Life could not be so cruel.

"You're . . . you're . . ." He couldn't say *exquisite*, he couldn't say *ravishing*. One simply didn't to a young lady one hadn't even been introduced to. Hell, he couldn't have said anything at all, not past the lump in his throat. Forrest thought of how she would have looked with a cloud of that hair floating over her warm, glowing skin, highlighting the golden flecks in her greenish eyes, and he nearly moaned out loud. Enough for a small dog, the hair would have come well over her shoulders, maybe to her waist, veiling her—oh, God. Not that she wasn't adorable as she was, with shaggy curls like a halo framing her lovely face. The curls gave her a pixieish look, a fresh, young innocence. "My God, you're a child!"

Sydney raised her chin. "I am eighteen, Mr. Randall."

"Eighteen?" Now the viscount did groan. "At eighteen females who look like you shouldn't be allowed out of the house without an armed guard!

And where do you go, missy, leaving your sturdy footman outside, but into a nest of thieves?"

Oh, dear, Sydney thought, he was getting angry again. "Please, Mr. Randall, I only need—"

"You need a better haircut." Forrest almost bit his tongue for saying that. What he was going to say was "You need a spanking," which only sent his rattled brain reeling in another direction. He compromised with: "You need a keeper. And I am not Randall, for heaven's sake."

"Oh, I am sorry." And Sydney was sorry their conversation had to end; she was finding this man a fascinating study, almost like a new species. "Could I speak with Mr. Randall?"

"He's, ah, tied up at the moment. I'm Mayne."

Sydney bowed slightly in her seat. "How do you do, Mr. Mean, er, Mayne. I am Miss—"

He held his hand up. "No names, please. The walls have ears, you know." He also knew that deuced door was partly open.

Sydney nodded wisely, humoring the man. He was obviously dicked in the nob. She could hear grunts and thuds coming from the connecting room as well as he.

"Newlyweds next door." He shrugged, then almost blushed at her blank look. Gads, he wasn't used to such innocence. Which reminded him again of the hobble the chit had nearly landed in, a little lamb prancing into the wolves' lair. "Miss, ah, miss, I am sure you think your situation is dire, but coming here is not the solution."

Sydney was confused. "If you can't go to a moneylender for a loan, where can you go?"

Forrest dragged his hands through his hair again. He vowed never to introduce this featherbrain to his mother. "Let us start over again, shall we? Has no one warned you that moneylenders are unscrupulous?"

She nodded, and he looked pleased. "Has no one warned you that you end up paying, and paying again, far more than you borrow?"

She nodded once more. Mr. Mayne seemed almost pleasant now. "And finally, has no one warned you that moneylenders are the last resort of even hardened gamblers?" He was positively grinning, a lovely boyish grin despite the rumpled, battered look. He had nice eyes too, she thought, May-sky blue and not the least bit shifty. Why had no one warned her that moneylenders could be such handsome rogues?

6

Cads and Collateral

"*B*ut I only need a thousand pounds, Mr. Mayne."

He didn't think to correct her about his title. The determined little baggage must be the only female in London not conversant with his office, income, and expectations, and some devil in him wished to keep her that way. As infuriatingly pig-headed as the chit was, at least she wasn't simpering and toadying up to him. Besides, there were more important misconceptions to remedy. He thought he could depend on the stalwart-seeming footman to see they were not interrupted.

"A thousand pounds? That's a great deal of money, you know." It fairly boggled his mind to consider what she could have done to require such a sum. Unfortunately, simply by being where she was the wench proved nothing was too preposterous for Miss Sydney Lattimore. Ridiculous name for a girl anyway. But "A thousand pounds?"

"I really wish you would stop treating me like a wayward child, Mr. Mayne. I do know what I am

52

about." His raised brows expressed skepticism. "I haven't undertaken this move lightly, I can assure you," she went on, determined to erase that patronizing half smile. "I do know it's not at all the thing for a young female to conduct such business, and I did have sense enough to wear Mama's old mourning clothes so no one would recognize me. But my circumstances absolutely require such funds."

"And you couldn't go to your father or brother or banker for aid, like any proper female?"

"I do not have any of those," she said quietly, bravely, bringing a pang of . . . something to the viscount's heart. He prayed it wasn't knight-errantry.

"You must have some family, someone."

"Of course I do, that's why I need the loan. I have a plan."

The viscount didn't doubt it for a moment. He steepled his hands and prepared to be entertained. Miss Lattimore didn't disappoint him. Her plan was no more mercenary than that of any mama planning to fire her darling off in society, hoping to land a prize in the marriage mart.

"So you see, if Winnie weds Baron Scoville—oh, no names. If my sister marries a certain warm gentleman, then we can repay the loan and not have to worry about the future."

So it was Scoville the sisters had in their sights. The baron was rich and wellborn, a worthy target, the viscount believed, if too proper by half for his, Forrest's, own liking. The self-righteous prig was never going to ally himself to any penniless nobody from a havey-cavey household though; he held his own value too dear. "Barons can generally look as high as they wish for a bride, you know," Forrest said, trying to be polite.

Sydney lifted her straight little nose anyway. "The La—we are not to be despised, sir. Mother's brother was an earl and my grandfather is a very well-respected military gentleman. We do have some connections; what we don't have is the where-withal to take advantage of them. Besides, the baron has already paid my sister particular attention."

General Lattimore, by George. So the chit was quality. She just might pull it off. Especially if . . . "Is your sister as pretty as you?"

Sydney laughed, showing enchanting dimples. "Me? Oh, no, Winifred is beautiful! And she is sweet and kind and always behaves properly and knows just what to say even to the most boring curate. She does exquisite needlework and has a pleasing voice. We've never had a pianoforte, but I am certain Winnie would excel at it. She's—"

"A perfect paragon," the viscount interrupted, "who would make a delightful wife for any man, especially a rich one. You have convinced me. How do you propose to convince the mark—er, the man?"

Miss Lattimore did not need to reflect on the matter; she had it all worked out. She smiled again, and something about those dimples and the sparkle in her eyes made Forrest forget to listen to her rambling recitation about dresses and receptions and music lessons. "For the polite world seems to feel a lady should be musical. I do not see why myself, if she has so many other accomplishments, but the baron never fails to compliment my cousins on their playing. I am certain Winnie can do as well."

Sydney was satisfied that she had presented her

case in a reasonable, mature fashion. She would have been furious to know the viscount hadn't heard a word. He was too worried about his own urge to go slay all of Miss Lattimore's dragons. No, that kind of chivalry was dead and well-buried. He would not get involved, not past warning the maiden to stay out of the paths of firebreathers.

"Have you considered what would happen if you borrow the money, rig your sister out like a fashion plate, and still do not bring the baron up to scratch? How would you repay the loan, considering it will be far higher than when you started, due to the exorbitant interest rates?"

Sydney chewed on her lower lip, adorably. The viscount bit his. "You are still thinking about the Motthavens," she said.

He wasn't, not at all. "The, ah, cents-per-centers feel strongly about getting their blunt back."

"Of course you do, you couldn't stay in business else. I do have other strings to my bow. There are other men, of course. They might not have as deep pockets as the baron, but I feel certain they would repay the debt to have Winnie as their bride. Moreover, I do not intend to use the full thousand pounds on Winnie's clothes. It would hardly cover a court dress, for one thing, though we do not aim so high. Naturally you wouldn't know about such matters."

The viscount knew all too well about dressmakers' bills and the costs of entertaining. A thousand pounds was not nearly enough for a chit's presentation Season. His sisters' balls had each cost more than that for one night's show. He passed over Miss Lattimore's assumption of his ignorance of the ton and focused on the convolutions of her great plan. "So that I might be clear on all the details," he asked, "precisely how, then, do you intend to outfit the sacrificial virgin?"

Sydney resented his sneering expression and high-handed tones. "My good man," she replied in Aunt Harriet's most haughty manner, "I shall use a portion of the money on *my sister*, and invest the rest. My earnings shall be enough to see us through the Season, and yes, even repay the loan if Winnie cannot like any of her suitors. There is no question of a sacrifice."

The chit continued to amaze him. "Do you mean," he practically shouted, "that you intend to borrow money at twenty percent or higher and invest it in what? Consols or such? At less than five? No one could be so crack-brained!"

"I'll have you know that I have ways of doubling my money, sirrah. That is fifty percent!"

"It is a hundred percent, you widgeon! That's why women should never handle money. You—"

"You made me nervous by shouting," she said quietly, accusingly.

Damn. She wasn't the only one rattled, if he could yell at a slip of a girl. "I apologize. Pray tell, though, if you have such a sure way to capitalize on an investment, why don't you take it to a bank? They are always eager for new ventures. They give fair rates of interest and plenty of advice."

She did not sound quite as smug. "It is not that kind of investment. I intend to wager on an exhibition of fisticuffs."

Sam Odum's club must have done more damage than the viscount knew; this had to be a fevered dream wherein a budding incomparable could spout the most skitter-witted nonsense with the serene confidence of a duchess. He really tried not to shout this time. His voice came out more a hoarse croak: "You're going to gamble your future on a mill?"

"Put like that, it does sound foolish, but it's not just any mill, er, match. There is a boxer, a Hollander, who has established a certain reputation and therefore high odds. My footman, Wally, is scheduled to take him on in a few weeks, and we have every confidence of Wally's victory." Sydney was on firm ground now that she had the usurer's attention. She should have saved her breath about Winnie and the baron and gone right to the boxing with a man like Mr. Mayne. One look at him, his broad shoulders and well-muscled legs, should have told her he'd be more absorbed in fisticuffs than fashion. Perhaps his line of business even required a degree of skill in the sport. "No one in Little— where we lived has ever been able to beat Wally, and he's been training especially hard now. He'll win."

Viscount Mayne was indeed a follower of the Fancy. "Do you mean the Dutch champion they call the Oak? I heard he was to fight again soon. And Wally's the big fellow outside? He might have a chance if he's as good as you say. The Oak has gone to fat, I've heard."

"No, that's Willy outside, Wally's twin. Willy can't box; he has a glass jaw."

Forrest sighed. "Don't you know anything about defense? The fellow is there to protect you; you don't tell the enemy about his weaknesses."

"Oh. I didn't know you were my enemy. I thought we were simply discussing a loan."

"Right, the loan. Well, Miss, ah, miss, what would you put down as collateral?"

"Collateral?"

"Yes, you know, as guarantee for the loan. Loans are often secured with a mortgage, the title to a piece of property, a race horse or even a piece of jewelry. Something of equal value that the lender gets to keep if the loan is not satisfied."

"Oh, but I intend to repay every farthing."

"They all do, the pigeons Randall plucks. You see, no one is going to issue an unsecured loan to a schoolgirl."

"I am *not* a schoolgirl! And that's gammon, for my maid Annemarie said gentlemen write out vouchers all the time for loans, on their word of honor alone."

"Precisely. Gentlemen. On their word of honor."

Instead of becoming discouraged, Miss Lattimore got angry. "I have as much honor as any man. I'll have you know my family name has never been touched by ignominy, and it never shall in my lifetime. I resent any implication to the contrary, Mr. Mayne, especially coming from one in your position. Why, I'd sooner trust my word to repay a loan than I would yours not to cheat me on the terms. So there." And she pounded the chair arm for emphasis the way the general did, and nearly fell off her seat when the arm wasn't there. The dastard was grinning.

"You have definitely made your point, Miss, ah, Lamb. I—"

"And I resent your comparing me to that notorious female. I am trying to help my family in the only way I know how. I am not trying to make a spectacle of myself."

The viscount stroked his chin. "I rather had in mind one of those cute, curly little creatures who gambol into quicksand."

Sydney fingered her uneven curls. "I did it myself."

"I never would have guessed. But I cannot keep calling you Miss Ah if we are going to be partners."

"Partners? We are?" Sydney didn't care if he called her Misbegotten, if he would lend her the money! "Oh, thank you!"

Lend it he would, and most likely was always going to. The viscount was acting against all of his better judgment . . . and bowing to the inevitable. Giving her the blunt was the only way to keep the minx out of—"Yes, Mischief, I am going to give you the money, but with conditions."

Sydney eagerly drew a pencil and a scrap of paper out of her reticule. "Yes, sir, what is the rate? Shall you want payment in installments or one lump sum? I can figure out a schedule, or reinvest from the dress allowance or—"

"Hold, Mischief. I said *give*. Consider it a parting gift from O. Randall and Associates." He ignored the louder thumps from the other room and pushed the leather purse with the thousand pounds over to her. "That way neither of us is ensnared. You know, 'neither a borrower nor a lender be.' "

She shook her head, sending curls every which way. The devil was quoting Scripture again. "And you say women have no head for business. You cannot just give away a sack of gold to a stranger."

"Why not? It's mine. My brother had some gaming debts."

"And you collected from your own brother?"

The viscount didn't bother refuting fustian. He pushed the purse a little closer.

Sydney could almost feel the weight of the coins, but she could not reach out those few inches for the sack. "I do not mean any offense, Mr. Mayne, but a lady cannot accept such a gift. There are certain standards of which you may not be aware, but it would be highly improper. Flowers, perhaps, but a thousand pounds?"

The viscount laughed out loud, even though it hurt his sore jaw and disturbed his ribs. "Doing it too brown, my girl. If you can dress up in your mother's clothes and go to the Greeks, talking about boxing matches like they were afternoon teas, then you can take the money. It's too late to stand on your uppers, Mischief." He got up and put the sack in her lap. "Besides, I have a secret to tell you. I am not really a moneylender."

Sydney looked at the bag of money in her lap, the rumpled man with the lopsided grin, the shambles of an office with the sign on the door. She nodded. She had the money; she could humor the Bedlamite.

"I am a viscount."

"And I am the queen of Persia. Therefore I shall have no problem repaying you by the end of the Season." She stood to leave.

"But you haven't heard my conditions yet."

He was standing quite close to her, still wearing that devilish smile. Sydney sat down. "Of course, the rates."

He waved that aside. "I said you needn't repay the deuced loan; I certainly would not make profit on it. Even we viscounts have some standards. But here are my terms: the first is that you never, ever try to contact another loan shark. You contact me and only me if you find yourself in difficulty again." He scrawled his Grosvenor Square address on her piece of paper. "Next, you never return here, no matter how many musclebound footmen you have. Promise me on your honor, Mischief, and your family name that you prize so highly."

He was no longer grinning. Sydney solemnly swore and he smiled like the sun coming out again. "Good. And finally, I get to keep the hair."

"As collateral? But it's not worth nearly enough."

It was to him.

Sydney stood by the door, cradling a sack of currency instead of a basket of hair, and vowing again to repay the reckoning. Up close, Forrest got a hint of lavender mixed with the camphor and he could almost count the freckles across the bridge of her nose.

"You know, my dear," he said, keeping his voice low, "if you have trouble meeting the obligation, I am sure we could find some mutually satisfying way of settling accounts."

There was that wide-eyed stare of muddled incomprehension. Miss Lattimore hadn't the faintest idea of what he was shamefully suggesting. So he showed her. Tenderly, he placed his lips on hers and softly kissed her.

Oddly enough, Sydney was not frightened. It was all of a piece for this incredible afternoon. In fact, it was quite enjoyable, being held in a man's arms and sweetly kissed. All the other men of her acquaintance—not many, to be sure, and more boys than men—smelled of bay rum or talc, soap or sandalwood. This one smelled of . . . sweat. And the smell was as wild as the man, disturbing and exciting and—a cad! Sydney struggled and he released her immediately. Smiling.

"You . . . you," she sputtered. "You were right. Moneylenders *are* vermin." And she slapped him.

Sydney was horrified. She'd never struck a man before. Then again, she'd never been kissed before, nor been offered a slip on the shoulder. She knew she was partially to blame for being where no lady should be. Of course a gentleman would not have taken advantage of a lady no matter what the circumstances, but Mr. Mayne, or whoever he was, was not a gentleman. She should not have expected him to act like one, nor reacted so violently when he did not. Sydney was prepared to apologize, when the door burst open.

Willy shoved his way in, ready to do battle after the noises he'd heard. He saw his mistress looking irresolute, saw the five-fingered calling card she'd left on the handsome devil's grinning face. He shook his head. "I told you and told you, Missy, not with your open hand." He smashed his fist right in the viscount's eye with enough force to ensure a spectacular shiner.

Forrest raised his hands in submission. He knew he was wrong to steal the kiss, but it was well worth it. He smiled, remembering.

"And if that don't work," Willy continued, "we taught you what to do." He kneed the viscount in the groin.

Miss Lattimore stepped over his lordship daintily, swearing to have the money back and wishing him good day.

Forrest groaned. Women.

7

Fils et Frères

*T*he Lattimore sisters were in funds and the
Mainwaring brothers were nearly identical again.

Before leaving the Fleet Street premises, Viscount Mayne staggered to the doorway of the adja-
cent room and told the occupants: "Listen up, you
bounders. I just made a donation to a worthy cause
on your behalf. A thousand pounds of charity ought
to buy you a better seat on the boat to hell. Unless
you want that lucky day to come soon, you bastards
best remember everything I said, and forget everything you heard."

Then he gathered his coat—London would just
have to see the immaculate viscount in his shirt-
tails for once—and his misused cravat. He picked
up the carpetbag of weaponry and Miss Lattimore's
basket. On reflection he decided he was going to
look enough like a bobbingblock without a little
wicker handle slung over his arm. Removing the
mound of hair, he carefully wrapped it in that
vastly utilitarian item, his soiled neckcloth.

Forrest entered Mainwaring House through the rear door. One of the scullery maids dropped a bowl of beans, the turnspit dog growled, and Cook threw her apron over her head, wailing.

The viscount slunk off to the study, where he penned out notes to accompany the canceled IOUs. *This matter has been attended to,* he wrote. *Best wishes for your future, Yrs., etc. Vct. Mayne.* He did not feel he owed the flats any further explanation, nor did he think they would pay attention to any advice he might give about the folly of dipping too deep. He placed the notes with a footman, then finally placed himself in the hands of his father's top-lofty valet. That worthy's already pasty complexion took on a greenish cast when confronted with this latest Mainwaring casualty. Heavens, Findley thought. Did they never win?

After a long soak in a hot tub, a nourishing meal, and half a bottle of the duke's Burgundy, the viscount took to his bed for a long night's rest. He awoke—and instantly declared that was miracle enough for the day. He felt, and looked, worse than he had since a cannonball sent him flying off the HMS *Fairwind*'s deck, ending his naval career.

He couldn't bear to stay inside, where the housemaids tiptoed around him, their eyes averted. He didn't dare go outside, where children could get nightmares from a look at his face, horses might bolt, ladies swoon. He had to get out of the London fishbowl.

As soon as his brother was declared fit to travel, Forrest bundled Brennan into the coach for the ride to Sussex. He and Bren would be better off recuperating in the country under their mother's tender care. There would be fewer questions, at any rate.

They could give out that there had been a carriage accident. Or two.

Two beefsteaks for Wally every morning, for his training. Three cases of the general's favorite port. Enough macaroons and almond tarts and seed cakes for the legions of morning callers and afternoon teas. A small dinner party for Lord Scoville? No, that would be too coming. Besides, she'd have to invite Aunt Harriet.

Sydney was making lists and spending money. What joy! She and her sister had already been to the Pantheon Bazaar where, Annemarie the maid informed them, they could get the best bargains on ribbons and lace and gloves and stockings. The Lattimore ladies had patronized fabric warehouses, plumassiers, milliners, and shoemakers. They had *not* visited a single dressmaker, saving money as fast as they spent it. Annemarie's émigré connections could whip up the most fetching outfits, *à la mode* and meticulously crafted, for a quarter of the price of a haughty Bond Street modiste. Annemarie herself was a wizard with a needle, changing a trimming here, a mesh overskirt there. She removed ribbons and sewed on spangles, making each of the girls' gowns appear as many.

At Sydney's insistence, most of the attention and expense was devoted to her sister's wardrobe. No one noticed the little sister anyway, when Miss Lattimore was such a beauty. Winifred went out more, too. She did not seem to mind interminable visits with Aunt Harriet and Trixie, while Sydney preferred to stay home, reading the newspapers to the general and reveling in every gossip column's mention of the new star rising on the social horizon.

Sydney did allow herself to be persuaded to purchase a dress length of jonquil muslin, which then required the most dashing bonnet she'd ever owned: a cottage straw with a bouquet of yellow silk daisies peeping from under the brim, two russet feathers a shade darker than her hair curling along her cheek, and green streamers trailing down her back and under her chin. It looked elegant, sophisticated, alluring—more so once she had her ragged locks trimmed by a professional coiffeur.

"Oh, Sydney, your beautiful hair," Winifred cried. "And you did it for me!"

Sydney thought that cutting her hair was the least of what she'd done. She would never discuss her visit to Fleet Street with her sensitive sister, though, especially not this afternoon, when Winnie was due to go for a drive in the park with Baron Scoville. Sydney couldn't trust the watering pot not to have a *crise de nerfs* right in front of him.

"Hush, you peagoose," Sydney teased. "We can't have the baron see you with swollen eyes and a red nose. He might think you the kind of woman to be enacting him scenes all the time. No gentleman would like that." She did not add, *Especially one so concerned with his consequence as the baron.* Winnie seemed pleased by the attention of the self-important peer; far be it from Sydney to disparage such a well-breeched gentleman.

"Besides," she said, "I did not cut my hair for you. I always hated that impossible mop. It weighed down my head and would never take a curl. Now I couldn't make it lay flat if I wanted to, and I feel free of all that heaviness and constant bother. Look at me. I am almost fashionable! You better be careful I don't steal all of your beaux away!"

"You could have all the admirers you want, dearest, if you would just go out and about more. Why, the gentlemen will flock to your feet when they see you in your new bonnet. You can have your pick!" Winnie giggled, her spirits restored. "Maybe one of the Bond Street fribbles will catch your fancy."

Sydney didn't think so.

The Duchess of Mayne was a student of breeding. She had intricate charts of the bloodlines of her dogs, their conformations, colors, temperaments. When she selected a mating pair, she was fairly certain of the results. Hers was the most noted establishment for Pekingese dogs in the kingdom. Lady Mayne was proud of her dogs.

She herself collected seeds from the best blossoms in her garden, for next year's blooms. Her gardens were mentioned in guidebooks. She was proud of her flowers.

She should have stopped there.

In the middle years of her marriage, when Lady Mayne still discussed her marriage at all, she used to boast that her husband could accuse her of many things, but never infidelity. All four of her children had his dark hair and the Mainwaring nose. (Fortunately the girls had pleasing personalities and large dowries.) She used to say that blood would tell, that breeding was all. She used to be proud of her sons, tall and straight, darkly handsome, like two peas in a pod.

Like two peas in a pod that had been left on the vine too long, stepped on by the farmer's hobnail boots, then run over by the farm cart.

"This is why I sent you to London? This is how you help your brother and keep the family name from the tattle-mongers? This is how you were raised to behave?"

If Forrest had expected loving kindness and tender sympathy from his mother, he was disabused of that notion as soon as he helped Brennan past the front door. The duchess didn't even wait for the servants to retreat before lighting into her eldest offspring.

"This is what comes from letting you go off to the navy. You did not learn violence with your mother's milk! It's all that man's fault, I swear. There has never been so much as a soldier in my family. The Mainwarings were ever a belligerent lot, so proud of tracing their roots to William the Conqueror. Merciful heavens, who wants to be related to a bloodthirsty conqueror? And all of those kings' men and cavalry officers your father's always nattering on about, that's where you got this streak of brutality. And you are supposed to be the sane and sober one, the heir. Heir to your father's lackwits, I'd say. A diplomat, he calls himself. Hah! If he was ever around to teach his sons diplomacy, they wouldn't behave like barroom brawlers and look like spoiled cabbages!"

"Thank you, Your Grace," Forrest teased, trying to coax her into better humor. His mother hadn't been in a rant like this since last Christmas, when the governor came down to visit. "I am pleased to be home, too."

Brennan was grinning as best he could around the sticking plaster, since it was his brother under fire. Then the duchess turned that fond maternal eye, and scathing tongue, in his direction.

"You!" she screamed as if a slimy toad had arrived in her entry hall. "You are nothing but a womanizer. A drunkard. A gambler. Up to every tomfoolery it has been mankind's sin to invent! You are even more harebrained than your brother, associating with such riffraff. You"—her voice rose an octave—"inherited your father's dissipations."

Bren tried to reason with the duchess; Forrest could have told his brother he was making a mistake, but he'd suffered enough pulling Bren's chestnuts out of the fire. Let the stripling dig himself in deeper. "Cut line, Mother," Brennan started. "You know the governor ain't in the petticoat line, never has been. And he don't play more than a hand or two of whist or drink overmuch. Gout won't let him. Besides, this last scrape wasn't all my fault."

"Of course not, you're too stupid to get into so much trouble on your own! I know exactly who is to blame. When I get my hands on that—"

"As a matter of fact, Mother, none of it would have happened if you had let me join the army as I wanted."

"Are you saying it is *my* fault?"

Forrest moved to stand in front of the buhl table; he'd always admired that Sèvres vase on it.

"Of course not, Mother. It's just that, well, London's full of chances to drink and gamble and, yes, meet that kind of woman. There's nothing much else to do."

"My dogs have better sense. You are supposed to spend your time in town at parties and museums and plays and picnics, meeting the *right* kind of woman. And as for the army, you lobcock, you can't even keep yourself in one piece in London! Imagine what might happen to you in Spain. Go to your room."

"Go to my room? You cannot send me to the nursery like a child, Mother. I am twenty-two."

"And you can come down to dinner when you act it."

Bren wasn't in shape to put on the formal clothes the duchess required at her table, nor make the long trek up and down the arched stairways. Still, to be dismissed like a schoolboy in short pants rankled. "But, Mother . . ."

The duchess picked up a potted fern from the sidetable. Bren left.

Lady Mayne turned to her eldest. "I'm going, I'm going," he surrendered, starting for the stairs to help Brennan.

"And I," she pronounced, still holding the plant, "am going to the greenhouse."

Forrest spun around and dashed down the hall after her. "Not the greenhouse, Mother! Not all that glass!"

A few hours later the duchess relented. Maybe she had been too hard on Forrest. He had brought Brennan home, after all. She decided to forgive him and listen to the whole story, perhaps hearing some news of the duke. She would even bring Forrest a cup of one of her special brews of tea. The poor boy looked like he needed it.

When the duchess knocked on Forrest's door and received no answer, she thought he might be sleeping. She turned the handle and tiptoed in to check. The bed was empty, so he must be feeling better. She'd just go along to Brennan's room to see how he was faring.

On her way out, the duchess chanced to catch sight of a foul piece of linen on her son's otherwise immaculate dresser. She knew that new valet of his was a slacker! Not in her house, Lady Mayne swore, yanking on the bellpull. She went to pick up the offending cloth, to demand its immediate removal, and that of the person responsible. Sweet mercy, the linen was bloodstained, and wrapped around . . .

If Forrest thought going down to Sussex would have stopped the talk in London, he was wrong. The duchess's shriek could have been heard in Hyde Park. If he thought his injuries would heal quicker in the country, he was wrong. Flying up those stairs did not do his ribs any good. Taking a flying teacup on the ear did not do his face any good. Listening to his mother berate him in front of his valet, the butler, two footmen, a housemaid, and his grinning brother did not do his composure any good.

And that was *after* the duchess realized the bundle was a woman's hair and not a Pekingese pelt.

"Well, old boy," the viscount told Nelson in the cold dower house library, "it's just you and me again." And a bottle of Madeira. "You're the wastrel and I'm the womanizer. No, I'm the ruffian and the rake. You're just the rat catcher."

Tarnation, how could his own mother think he'd ever take up the life of a libertine? Gads, that's the last vice he'd pick. Of course, he'd never met a woman like Mischief before. She was an exasperating little chit, he recalled with a smile, but pluck to the backbone and loyal to a fault. And a beauty. He'd like to get a look at the sister, Forrest mused. Maybe he would, if Scoville dropped the handkerchief. Forrest didn't travel in the same circles as the baron, but sooner or later he would meet the peer's bride.

He doubted he would ever meet Miss Sydney again. She'd move heaven and earth to get the money back to Mainwaring House, he was sure, but he wouldn't be there. And he never went to debutante balls or such, so that was that.

He shut the book on Miss Sydney Lattimore and he shut his eyes, but he couldn't get those silly coppery curls out of his mind, or her quicksilver dimples or the way she nibbled on her lip before saying something outrageous. Zeus, she was always saying something outrageous. Forrest poured out another glass of wine and spilled some in a dish for Nelson. The viscount didn't like to drink alone.

What was going to happen to the widgeon? he pondered. She'd make micefeet of her Season for certain, landing in some scandalbroth or other. It would be a miracle, in fact, if Sydney's rackety ways didn't scare off that fop Scoville. On the other hand, maybe there was an intelligent *parti* not looking to rivet himself to a milk-and-water miss. He'd snap up Sydney Lattimore before she could say "I have a plan," debts and dowry or not.

What a dance she'd lead the poor sod. Forrest took another sip. Nelson belched. "You're right. We're a lot better off out of it," he told the hound. "We'll never see her after this anyway."

Wrong again.

8

By-blows and Blackmail

$\mathcal{V}$iscount Mayne had also been wrong when he called the Ottos bastards. Only one was. The other was his legitimate half-brother. Otto Chester, the ivory tuner, was actually the natural son of one Lord Winchester Whitlaw and his cook at the time, Mrs. Bella Boggs. No one knew the whereabouts of Mr. Boggs. Lady Whitlaw was less than pleased. Since his wife held both the reins and the purse-strings in that marriage, Lord Whitlaw watched as Bella was tossed out in the cold on her *enceinte* ear. Before she got *too* cold, though, Lord Whitlaw sent her to his Irish estate, where Lady Whitelaw never visited. Before Bella grew too big with child, Whit-law married her off to Padraic O'Toole, his Irish estate manager.

The infant was named Chester O'Toole. He took after his father, being pale and thin and feckless. He also inherited his father's left-handedness, to Paddy O'Toole's bile at the continual reminder. The boy was sent to England at his father's expense, to receive an education befitting the son of a lord. Being weak and puny and a bastard, he quickly learned cowardice and subterfuge.

Randy O'Toole was Chester's legitimate half-brother, born on the right side of the blanket. Presently using the name of Otto Randall, financial consultant, Randy was also presently bound and gagged in his side office, next to Chester.

The younger O'Toole resembled *his* father, with the same red hair, stocky stature, and vile temper. (The Duchess of Mayne would have been pleased with this true breeding of bloodlines.) Randy was also well educated at Lord Whitlaw's—unwitting—expense, thanks to Paddy's fancy work with the estate books. Randy turned out to have his sire's flair for figures. The crookeder the better.

Bella never had life so good, there in Ireland. For the first time in her life she did not have to work. Indeed, as the manager's wife, she could lord it over the lesser employees and socialize far above her station. She had two sons with futures, a husband who provided well, a cozy kitchen all her own. And she owed everything to Lord Whitlaw.

So grateful was Bella, in fact, that she bore his lordship another child, another colorless, stringy left-hander. This child was a girl, who now plied a trade on the streets of Dublin, lest her mother's heritage be forsaken.

Paddy was furious, but what could he do? His job paid too well to leave and his wife was too well liked by the boss to beat. Paddy took to drink. He also took more and more money out of Lord Whitlaw's share of the estate and added it to his own account. Bella was better off, but not feeling as well blessed, with a surly, jug-bitten Irishman at her hearth.

Life went on. The children grew to young men and fallen woman. Bella grew stouter on her own cooking and Paddy grew meaner and the estate grew poorer, all of which may have contributed to his lordship's less frequent visits.

When he did chance to come north one fall for the hunting, Paddy followed him closer than his shadow, waiting for Whitlaw to come near Bella. More for loyalty's sake and the comfort of familiarity than anything else, Whitlaw did approach O'Toole's wife. In the stables, in the back parlor, on the kitchen table. That last was too much for Paddy. He challenged Lord Whitlaw to a duel.

Whitlaw refused. A gentleman did not duel with his social inferiors. Especially not if they were better shots. Then bare fists, Paddy insisted. Whitlaw turned craven—not a far turn at that—and threatened to call in the sheriff.

Now what could Paddy do? The estate was bled dry and Bella was free to anyone who wanted the immoral sow, for all Paddy cared. He shot Lord Whitlaw.

Paddy hung, of course. No low Irish land agent could get away with the hot-blooded murder of an English lord. Bella and the boys fled to England with the money before anyone thought to look into the estate books. O'Toole not being a good name to bear right then, neither in Ireland nor England, Bella took back her maiden name, Bumpers. The boys became Otto Chester and Otto Randall, since Bella determined that no one would suspect them of being brothers if they had the same first name. Also, it was easier to remember.

Bella used Lord Whitlaw's—unknown—bequest to establish herself as a respectable widow in Chelsea. Her sons went into business, O. Randall and Associates, Financial Consultants. Cardsharps and loansharks, limited.

Among certain circles, Lord Forrest Mayne was considered to be of careful intellect, a thoughtful man who brought his not inconsiderable powers of ratiocination to bear before forming a judgment. Among other circles he was simply called a "knowing 'un," and respected as such. One could only wonder what was going on in his mind for this downy cove to make so many false assumptions. He'd thought to bask under his mother's solace; he really should have known better. He concluded she was the most unnatural parent a grown man could have; he hadn't met Bella Bumpers. At least the duchess never kicked him while he was trussed up like a Christmas goose.

"My babies," Bella wailed when she entered the office on Fleet Street and found her sons tied and gagged. "My precious boys! How did this happen? How many cutthroats jumped on you?"

She got Chester's neckcloth out of his mouth first. "Mayne," he gasped.

"Mayne?" Bella's face turned red and her nostrils flared. Her chest swelled like a pouter pigeon's. Then she started kicking at Chester and beating him about the head with her reticule, which contained, as usual, a small pistol.

"Bud, Ma," Chester whimpered, trying to drag himself out of her way.

"Don't you 'ma' me, you gutless clunch. I don't want to be your ma anymore. I *never* wanted to be your ma. I even changed my name so I could pretend I wasn't your ma. I told you and told you to leave the little lordlings be. Pick on country grapeseeds, I said, new-blooming tulips, or raw army recruits. So what pigeon do you find to pluck, huh? Young Mainwaring, that's who! With big brother right here to protect him, like any jackstraw could have told you!

"And you," she screeched, aiming her next kicks at Randall, "you couldn't leave well enough alone. No, you had to set your bully-boy on the sprig. Where is that dung heap anyway? I'll tear him limb from limb for this!"

Bella hadn't taken the gag from Randy, so Chester tried to answer: "Mayne had him pred-ganged."

"What's wrong with you?" Bella's beady little eyes narrowed.

"I fing my node id broke."

"Oh, yeah?" She screwed his head around toward a better angle, squinting at the questionable fixture. "Yeah, it is." She put her knee on Chester's chest and wrapped her fat fingers around his nose. Then she yanked. "Now it ain't. Bad enough you look like some corpse without you sniffing at your ear for the rest of your life."

While Chester was unconscious, she untied Randall, after getting in a few more kicks. "So what did he do to you, fleabrain?"

Randy wouldn't say. He just shook his head.

"What's the matter, runt? Cat got your tongue?" Bella cackled, then peered at him. "Nah, Mayne's known for a gentleman. He'd never carve a man up like that, not even a little maggot like you."

"My teeth are mithing. I thwear I'll kill the bathtard."

"That ain't no way to talk about your brother. 'Sides, he just gulled the flat. The duke would of coughed up the reckoning. You're the one what ordered him worked over, not Chester."

"Not Chethter. Forretht Mayne. I'm going to thee him dead."

"I always said your bark was bigger'n your bite. Ha-ha!" Sympathy was not one of Bella's strong points. "You're just lucky they didn't set the magistrate on us for what you done."

"The deuthed codth head threatened to do jutht that. That'th why I—"

"Oh, shut up already. You sound just like your father at his last prayers."

Since Padraic O'Toole's last prayers were spoken through a hood with a noose around his neck, Randy shut up.

Bella was shaking her head. "You two together have about as much brains as the average pullet. All that schooling, and you didn't even learn to listen to your ma. I told you time and time again about quality and family. You know, how some of them watch out for kinfolk just the way we look after each other."

A few days later the same little group was gathered at Bella's row house in Chelsea.

"Stop looking over your shoulder, Chester. Swells like Mayne hardly set foot out of Mayfair. 'Sides, he wouldn't recognize you anyways. I hardly do myself and I'm your mother. I ain't happy about that neither, but I can live with it."

"But, Ma, what are we going to do? We can't just stay here. I say we take what we have and set up on the Continent."

"Shut up, you pudding heart, we ain't running," his brother said.

Randy had false front teeth by now, fancy ivory ones taken from some dead nabob by the undertakers next door. They hurt like hell, which did not do much for his temper. The top set stuck out over his bottom lip, not doing much for his appearance either. "I still say we kill Mayne. Then we don't even have to relocate."

"That's the most harebrained idea I ever heard. Get that? Harebrained, rabbit-toothed?" Bella nearly fell off her chair, laughing so hard. When she stopped laughing she boxed Randy's ears until the false teeth flew out. "You got your father's same nasty temper. You want to end like him too? Like as not you will, but you ain't making gallows' bait out of me and Chester. Didn't you learn anything from your father? No one can kill a titled nob less'n he's got a higher title. They call that a fair fight. Or if he's got more money. They call that justice."

"And what about the money, Ma?" Chester asked. "How are we going to collect without Sam?"

"We've got enough of the ready for now. As for the slips His Nibs left us, a solicitor's letter with them big words like 'debtors' prison' ought to be just as encouraging as a visit from Sam."

"And what about that thousand pounds he gave away?" Randy wanted to know.

Bella's pudgy arms waved that aside. "We'll get

the blunt back easy enough. But this ain't about money, you blockheads. It's about revenge."

Chester started shaking but Randy smiled, looking more like a rabid rodent than anything else.

Bella's plan was simple: hit 'em where it hurt. Mayne's pockets were so deep, he wouldn't even feel the loss. His pride was another matter.

"We can get the money from that dandy Scoville anyway. Soon as he announces the engagement and can't back down from the wedding, we threaten to go to the gossip rags with word that his bride's family ain't all it should be. Shady dealings in backstreet offices and all. He'll pay quick enough to keep that quiet."

"But how are we going to know if he picks the right girl?" Chester was nervous. Chester was already packed. "We don't have the chit's name. Even if Mayne wouldn't kill me on sight, you know I'm not fit enough to go to the clubs to listen to the gossip."

"You're not fearless enough, you mean," Bella taunted. "Don't worry, chicken-liver, we won't ask you to go outside yet. We just have to read the gossip columns ourselves. If that pompous ass Scoville is sniffing 'round some filly, the papers'll know it. If not, you just have to follow the footman home from that prize fight to see where he goes."

"Me?"

"Well, Rabbit-face sticks out like a sore thumb, don't he?"

"I want to know about Mayne." Randy wanted to change the subject.

"Oh, we get to him through the other wench, the one with gumption. My kind of female, from what you say, conniving and crafty. Imagine if your sister'd had that kind of bottom. B'gad, she could have been some rich man's mistress by now. No matter, we find out who that little baggage is and wait till she's got her name on everybody's lips, which I misdoubt will take too long. If she don't do it herself, we help her along, like mentioning her betting on the mill. Then we shout it loud and clear that the high and mighty Viscount Mayne has ruined her. He compromised her all right and tight. A gentle-bred innocent what's blotted her copybook. Either he'll have to marry the hobbledehoy brat and be miserable the rest of his life, or he'll see his name dragged through the mud along with hers. That won't sit well with him, not with his notions of family honor and all. Of course, if none of that works . . ."

"We kill him."

"And run to the Continent."

9

Mills and Masquerades

"*I* swear I'm sick of this petticoat tyranny, Forrest. You've got to do something!"

Brennan stormed into his brother's study, interrupting to no one's displeasure an uncomfortable meeting between the viscount and one of his tenants. The farmer touched his brim and nodded to the younger lord on his way out.

"What was that about?" Bren asked, flopping into the chair just vacated.

"It was about the proper handling of randy young bulls. Whipslade can't seem to keep that Fred penned in, so I said I'd castrate him myself the next time he got into trouble." Forrest grinned. "Now, what was your complaint, little bull, er, brother?"

Bren got the hint. "But dash it all, Forrest, there's nothing to do!"

Forrest had plenty to keep him occupied, overseeing the vast Mainwaring holdings, to say nothing of checking all the London dailies for mention of acquaintances. Brennan's cracked ribs had kept him more confined to the house and his mother's carping, and he was fretting to be gone. He would have returned to London a se'night past, in fact, had the duchess not given strict orders to the stables forbidding him horse or carriage. No way was she letting him go back to the fleshpots of the city . . . or his father's house.

"You've got to talk to her, Forrest, convince her she's wrong about London."

"Dear boy, do I look that paper-skulled? I'd rather be keelhauled than tell the duchess she's wrong, thank you."

"Then the grooms. They will listen to you, Forrest," Brennan begged. "Deuces, they can't deny you your own cattle, can they? I know you wouldn't let me have the bays, but surely you'll lend me Old Gigi and the pony trap? The dog cart? How about a ride to the nearest posting house?"

For Brennan's sake, the viscount decided to make a short excursion to town. For Brennan's sake, he planned some harmless diversions, like a drive out to a prizefight at Islington two days later. They weren't doing *The Merchant of Venice* at Drury Lane, and he had to keep the boy entertained and out of trouble, didn't he?

They took the viscount's phaeton to Islington, with his matchless bays and his tiger Todd. Brennan half jokingly wondered why, if this was supposed to be his treat, he couldn't handle the ribbons. Todd nearly fell off his perch on the back, laughing.

They left town early to set an easy pace on account of Brennan's ribs—and the viscount's sworn word to his mother. As it turned out, they were none too early and had no chance of springing the pair with the roadway so clogged. All the sporting bloods were on their way to Islington, along with every other buck in town who was game for a wager. The upcoming bout had caught the attention and imagination of the entire male population of London, it seemed, and they were all on the road at once.

The Dutch champion was not called the Oak just because no one could pronounce his name. He had stood unbent through years of matches, never once being knocked to the canvas. Few men were cork-brained enough to meet him these days, so an exhibition of fisticuffs by the near legend was not to be missed. No one except the viscount knew much about the challenger, one Walter Minch. The word was he was undefeated in some shire or other, a young lad with size if no sense. Some claimed they'd seen him in training and he stripped to advantage. "Minch the Cinch" they dubbed him, hoping for better odds. Others swore he had to be a sacrificial shill for the bout's promoters. They weren't betting on his winning or losing, just on how long he stayed standing.

The viscount, of course, would have gone to the grave without divulging any foreknowledge of any footman's brother. He hoped and prayed Miss Lattimore's connection never came to light, much less his own. Not even his brother knew it was a servant named Willy who'd darkened Forrest's daylights, not the bloodsucker's hired killer. The viscount's eye was still sore; Wally stood a deuced good chance.

There were shouts, wagers, and rumors all along the slow drive. The clamor grew worse near the actual meeting grounds, naturally, as the drivers tried to thread their vehicles through the crowds to good vantage points. Todd jumped down to clear a path, and the viscount slid the bays between a racing curricle and a gig, with at least an inch to spare on either side. Then there were greetings and fresh odds, and everyone wanting to know the viscount's opinion, since he was known to be a follower of the Fancy himself.

Forrest smiled and told his eager listeners that since he'd never seen the man box, he couldn't make a fair guess. That's what they were all there for, wasn't it?

Anyone wishing an expert's advice before making his own wagers would have been wiser to follow the viscount around when he climbed down from the phaeton, leaving Todd at the horses' heads and Brennan with an ale in his hand.

Forrest greeted his friends, smiled at casual acquaintances, and ignored would-be hangers-on. The crowd was a mix of London gents, local gentry, neighborhood workingmen, pickpockets, and other riffraff. The viscount strolled about the grounds with no fixed purpose in sight, placing a wager here, making a bet there. He never put his name down for a lot of money, always denied knowing the new boxer. He shrugged good-naturedly about rooting for the underdog and took the long odds. The longer the better. If he'd staked all his blunt with one bookmaker, the odds would have swung considerably, with less profit for him—and Miss Lattimore.

Content, he ambled back across the field toward his phaeton, from whose high perch he'd have a clear view of the roped-off square. He was so satisfied with his transactions that he tossed a coin to an odd-looking clergyman standing on the perimeter of the crowd, clasping his Bible. "Say a prayer for Minch, Reverend," Forrest called over his shoulder.

The minister appeared as if St. Peter had just called his name off the rolls, but he hoarsely answered to the viscount's back: "Bless you, my son."

He was the last person you'd expect to see at a place like this, a holy man at a mill, and this was the last place Reverend Cheswick wanted to be. But if Cheswick had to be there—and Bella seemed adamant about that—then Chester was going in disguise. Randy tried to tell him that his own wishy-washy phiz with its newly bloated nose was the best camouflage, but Chester went out and got himself a bagwig, thick spectacles, and a moldy frock coat from the same source as Randy's choppers. The mortuary workers threw the Bible in free. Chester's identity was well hidden, in the one disguise guaranteed to draw attention to himself. He stuck out among the other men like a sore . . . nose. And wasn't it just his luck that the bastard who broke his nose had to be so bloody charitable? First Mayne gave away their thousand pounds and now he went out of his way to toss a golden boy to a man of the cloth. Chester supposed he was the type to encourage beggars with handouts too.

At least the worst was over. His disguise passed the test and now he could go home. He didn't have the information Bella wanted about where the footman lived or who he worked for, but she would have to understand. His pants were wet.

"Who was that rum touch you were talking to?" Brennan wanted to know.

"Who? Oh, the old quiz? Most likely some missionary come to save our souls. Why?"

"Something about him just looked familiar."

"I doubt you meet many religious sorts in the circles you travel," his brother noted dryly, passing over the hamper of food they'd brought from town.

Before they could do justice to the cold chicken and sliced ham and Scotch eggs and crusty bread, a roar went up from the crowd. The champion was coming. The Oak strode to the clearing. The ground almost shook with his every step. The spectators cheered themselves hoarse, then they passed around the bottles and flasks again.

The Oak waved to the crowd, turning toward all four compass points while his seconds set a footstool in his corner. His cape swirled around his massive frame. Next he removed the cloak and slowly repeated the move so they could all appreciate his naked upper torso. They did, howling and stamping their feet as muscle rippled over muscle every time he raised an arm.

The viscount held his looking glass to his eye. "The Dutchman seems heavier than the last time I saw him fight. I wonder if it's all muscle or if the weight might slow him down."

"Care to hazard your blunt on it?" Bren asked, forgetting he'd sworn off wagering, at least for the remainder of this quarter.

Since Forrest was already financing the chub until his next allowance, he declined. "But I'll take you up on the bet anyway. If the Dutchman wins, you get to drive the bays home."

"And if the Oak loses?" Brennan asked suspiciously.

"Then you go to Almacks like Mother's good little boy and do the pretty."

Bren looked at the sleek pair in front of him, then at the mighty boxer in the ring. He couldn't lose. "Done."

It was the contender's turn to enter the ring. The mob hooted and whistled. Lord Mayne focused his glass on the young blond giant and nodded his satisfaction. She hadn't said identical twin, but the challenger could have been Willy of the glass jaw—and the strong right. Wally handed his coat to his second, the butter-stamp Willy, and the audience took on a new frenzy. There was not an ounce of fat on Walter Minch, just taut muscle. In addition, he and his twin were right handsome English lads, not foreigners. Bets were changed, notes passed across carriages.

"How are you at the quadrille?" Forrest laughed at his brother's look of dismay, then turned his glass back to where Willy and the waterboy were arranging towels and buckets and—

The smile faded from the viscount's lips, to be replaced by the most colorful string of curses heard outside a navy brigantine. Brennan would have been impressed if he didn't fear for his brother.

"Are you hurt? Did someone toss something at the bays? Should I send for a doctor, Forry? Do you want to go home? Do you want to change your bet?"

"Shut up, you rattlepate, you're drawing attention. And if you ever call me Forry again, I'll use your guts for garters."

Attention? Bren looked around. Everyone else was watching the referee giving instructions. Brennan didn't know whether to fear for his brother's sanity or for his own life. The curses were lower now, more mumbled than spoken, and seemed to be mixed with smoke. Bren could pick out expressions like "sons of rutting sea serpents" and "flogging around the fleet."

Life with his parents having taught Bren much about the Mainwaring tempers, he thought he just might get down and visit with some friends from town. "A little closer view, don't you know?"

The viscount did not know about his brother's painful climb down from the high-perch phaeton, nor Bren's worried backward glance as he limped toward a rowdy pair of bucks in a racing curricle. He didn't pay any attention to the shouted rules of the match, and he did not notice when his looking glass slipped through numb fingers to the ground far below. All he noticed—and the image would be etched in his mind's eye forever, magnified or not—was the waterboy. A slight, scruffy lad he was, dressed in a loose smock and baggy britches tied up with rope. His face was dirty, as though someone had rubbed his nose in the mud, and a greasy woolen cap was pulled low over his curls. His bright coppery curls.

He was going to kill her. There was no question in Forrest's mind. He was going to take her pretty little neck in his two hands and wring it. After the bout. Then he'd deliver some home-brewed to Wally's glass jaw—he owed him that anyway—and he'd shatter whichever of Wally's bones the Oak left in one piece. After the bout. To act before would not be prudent, and the viscount was always discreet. To smash his way through the crowds the way he wanted to with a raging Red Indian war cry, to tear the threesome limb from limb starting with the bogus waterboy, just might draw a tad of attention to Miss Sydney Lattimore. Murdering her was his fondest desire; protecting her reputation had to come first.

If one hint, one inkling of her presence here reached the tattle-mongers, she would not have to worry about dresses or dowries. She'd never be received anywhere in London and no man could think of offering for her. A woman in britches? Fast didn't begin to describe the names she would be called, and her precious sister would be tarred with the same brush.

And if Sydney didn't know what could happen if this horde of drunks found out she was a woman, then Wally and Willy should have known. They were supposed to protect her, weren't they? Hell, he only kissed her, and look what it got him. The twins couldn't be stupid enough to bring her unless they were sharing one brain between the two of them; he'd find out if he had to tear their skulls open.

Sydney must have twisted them around her thumb, Forrest decided, the same way she wheedled the loan out of him when he had no intention of giving it. Damn and blast, how could she have been so mutton-headed as to jeopardize her life and her entire future this way, and after giving her word, too?

That wasn't quite true, he conceded. She'd sworn only to stay away from the cents-per-centers, not boxing matches or congregations of castaways. The viscount cursed himself for not getting the little fool's promise to *pretend* to be a lady. Then he cursed himself for getting involved in the first place.

10

Riot and Rescue

Her whole life and future depended on this match, and Sydney could not watch it. While the viscount seethed about her presence there, chewing the inside of his mouth raw, not the least of his aggravation stemmed from the fact of Sydney's viewing men's bare chests. Blister it, the only bare chest she should ever see was his—her husband's, he meant. He need not have worried. For the most part her eyes were closed. When she had to open them to perform her duties, Sydney was still oblivious to everything but the screaming, shouting men, the fumes from pipes, cigars, and spilled ale, the appalling sound of fist meeting flesh. The blood.

"Let's go home," she whispered in Wally's ear after the first round. He gave her a big grin and pulled the cap down lower over her eyes. The bout went on.

The match was being fought under the new boxing rules with twenty-five timed rounds, short rests between, and judges to make the final ruling of victory or defeat. The old-style contests saw no break and no finish until only one man stood. The only decision was on the part of the loser, deciding when to stay down.

The innovations sought to make boxing less a gory contest of brute strength, more a test of skills and science. The new format appealed most to gentlemen like the viscount, who sparred himself and appreciated neat footwork and clever defense as well as carefully aimed blows. The nearer elements of the crowd, however, those on foot surrounding the canvas ring, had come to see mayhem committed. These bloodthirsty masses did not appreciate the finesse of a fencing match. They booed and hissed at each rest period and pressed closer to where Sydney stood, nearly paralyzed, along the ropes.

In the early rounds, the boxers were evenly matched. Wally had more cunning and quicker timing. He could dance out of danger, watching for openings and getting in some solid blows of his own. The Dutchman had the advantage in reach and devastating power behind even a glancing blow from those massive fists. Wally kept moving; the Oak kept missing. When the Dutchman connected, he did more damage. Wally's blows barely rocked the Oak, though he got in twice as many of them.

Wally collapsed in his corner at the rests while Willy and Sydney wiped his face and ladled out cool water and advice. The Oak just stood and glowered. The crowd loved him.

In the middle rounds, Wally took a blow that sent him to the canvas. He valiantly got back to his feet, blood streaming from his nose, and the crowd started cheering for him for putting on a good show. The odds shifted again, and more wagers were recorded in the betting books. Those who'd bet on Wally to go ten rounds were happily collecting. Sydney clutched her bucket.

Wally got in a solid right in the very next round, then a left before he danced out of range. He quickly ducked back in under a flailing windmill to land another one-two combination, and still a third, to the mob's joy, spilling the Oak's claret for him, too.

By the nineteenth round, both fighters were slowed with exhaustion. Wally had visible bruises on his face and body and a swollen gash over one eye that was restricting his vision. He was still game, despite Sydney's pleas that he not get up the next time he went down. The Oak was using the breaks to catch his own breath. He'd never had to go so long with a challenger, and his lack of conditioning was showing in the labored breathing. His worried seconds advised him to end the match soon.

The Hollander opened the twentieth round with a surprise roundhouse punch that caught Wally flat-footed. Now Wally's other eyebrow was cut open and blood poured down his face. There was a vehement disagreement in the corner when Sydney tried to wrench the towel out of Willy's hands to throw it in the ring. The mob howled, to think they would be deprived of the bloodletting.

"What's going on, for pete's sake?" Bren asked, starting to climb back up to the phaeton's seat so he could see better. He was almost knocked to the ground by his brother's hurried descent.

"The waterboy's trying to stop the fight," Forrest shouted over the crowd's roar as he pushed and pummeled his way toward the ring.

"My God, they'll kill him," Bren called, automatically following in his brother's wake.

"No, they won't," Forrest said through gritted teeth. "That's my job."

The gong finally ended the round.

"Enough, Wally. I'm going to end the match."

"No, Missy," yelled Wally, and "You can't, Miss Sydney," bellowed Willy. At least the noise of the rabble masked her name.

"We have to, Wally! You can't see and you can hardly stand. You can't get out of his way, and that's slaughter! Give me the dratted towel!"

She reached for it, where Willy was using the cloth to staunch the blood. Wally was furious and adamant. "No!" he shouted, throwing his arms up.

Sydney should have listened to Wally the first time, for he certainly had strength left. Enough strength for one of those arms to catch Willy on his all too susceptible jaw. Willy collapsed at Sydney's feet like a house of cards.

Sydney was in a near panic, trying to decide what to do. Wally was half blind and his senses pain-dulled. Willy was out for the count. Crude voices were screaming at her and rough hands were reaching through the ropes. Heaven help us, she prayed.

Then strong arms grabbed her from behind and plucked her out of the ring. Sydney started to scream until she heard a gruff voice close to her ear say, "Stow it, Mischief."

She had never been so happy to see anyone in her life, and neither had the crowd. Mayne himself taking a part in a great contest was just about the icing on the cake. Their angry shouts turned into cheers. Sydney couldn't understand any of it, nor why her devout Christian prayers had been answered by a raging pagan war god breathing thunder, but she was content to let him take charge. She never doubted for a moment that Mr. Mayne was at home in Purgatory. She watched as he cleared Wally's vision with a few deft strokes and whispered some words of encouragement, like "I'll kill you myself if you don't get back out there." Wally grinned and met the bell. Barely taking his eyes off the fight, Mayne grabbed Sydney's bucket and tossed its contents over Willy.

Willy lifted his head, saw who was above him, mumbled, "Aw, gov, this ain't the time for revenge," and passed out again.

Mayne grabbed Sydney by the collar, giving her a good shake while he was at it, before thrusting the empty bucket into her hands. "Go fill it," he ordered. She ran.

A stupefied Bren reached the corner just as Willy opened his eyes again. "Uh, Forrest," Bren said, helping the twin to his feet, "mind if I ask a foolish question?"

"You've always done so before," his brother answered, his gaze fixed on the fighters. Wally was circling and dodging, wearing the Oak down even if he wasn't landing any blows.

"Uh, what are we doing here?"

"I thought that was obvious. We're watching a prizefight."

"But do you *know* these people?" he asked in disbelief.

"Thanks to you, dear brother, only thanks to you. Now you can repay the favor by taking my bays and getting the waterboy out of here. Send Todd back to me."

Now Brennan was even more convinced that his brother had brain fever. "The bays? That gutter-snipe?"

Willy was more alert. He knew what he'd seen the last time this angry cove was near his mistress. "You can't take her! I won't let you carry Miss—" Thanks to Sydney, Lord Mayne knew just where to hit the footman to stop his protests.

The multitudes cheered. Now they had two mills to watch! Brennan just gaped.

As soon as Sydney returned with the full bucket, she found herself thrust against another chest. Mayne made the introductions. "This is my nod-cock of a brother Brennan, and this," he said with a sneer, "is Sydney."

Brennan could tell, even through the strips still binding his ribs, that the waterboy didn't feel right. "But he's a—" he started to say.

Forrest grabbed his shoulder. "That's right," he ground out close to Brennan's ear, "she's a lady. Now get her the hell out of here before anyone else notices!"

A lady? Should he then try to hand this raga-muffin up to the carriage? Brennan stood indecisive by the phaeton.

"You'll give the whole thing away, you looby," Sydney hissed at him. "You wouldn't help a boy to mount, would you?" Once she had clambered up and Sydney realized how well she could see, she declared her intention of staying to watch.

Brennan sent Todd back to help the viscount and took up the reins, muttering about totty-headed females, if she thought *he* was going to cross his brother. Sydney poked him in the ribs.

"Ow." Then Bren had to concentrate on backing the bays out of the narrow spot, answering the shouts of the amazed neighboring spectators with information that the boy was a runaway and he was taking him off before they lost sight of him again. "Relative of one of Mayne's tenants. The mother is frantic. M'brother's always watching out for his people, don't you know."

Sydney waited for Bren to complete the delicate maneuvering and reach the nearly deserted road-way before ripping up at him. "How dare you carry me off against my will when I should be helping my friends, and then tell your friends I'm a truant schoolboy or something?"

Bren's attention was fixed on the horses. "Well, I had to tell them something; it was the first thing I could think of, other than telling them Forrest was saving the bacon for a ramshackle miss. And I can't see where you were doing your friends much good. Better to leave things in Forrest's hands. It usually is."

Sydney had no answer. She sat quietly, worrying at her lower lip.

"You ain't going to cry, are you, brat?" he asked after giving her a quick look.

"Of course not, you nimwit." She sat up straighter. "You really are as unpleasant as your brother."

"Uh, just out of curiosity, none of my business, don't you know, but how exactly do you know m'brother?"

If he didn't know about the loan of his own blood

97

money, Sydney wasn't going to tell him. "He did me a favor" was all she said.

Bren nodded, relieved. "That explains it, then. Best of good fellows, like I said." When she made a very unladylike snorting sound, he continued. "Made no sense otherwise. You're not in his usual style. Forrest don't go near debs, and you"—taking in her dirty face and stablehand's clothes, from the smell of her—"ain't some expensive high flyer."

Wouldn't he just be surprised at his brother's infamous offer to her, Sydney thought indignantly, not that she wanted to be considered a barque of frailty, of course. And as innocent as she might be, she could not imagine a thousand pounds being an inconsequential payment for a lady's favors. At least the rake put a high value on her charms, as opposed to the opinion of this paltry gamester. Sydney tilted her nose in the air and told him, "I'll have you know I wouldn't care to be your brother's usual anything, Mr. Mayne."

"Oh, I ain't Mayne. That's Forrest's title, not his name. I thought you knew." In fact Brennan could not imagine anyone not knowing. "I'm Mainwaring," he added.

"Then he wasn't lying and he really is a viscount? How sad."

Bren was confused enough. "I always thought being a viscount was a good thing. Not that I envied him, you know. Wouldn't want all those headaches."

Sydney meant it was sad that a noble family was so come down in the world that one son was a wastrel and the heir was reduced to earning a far from honorable living among low company. He must be successful at it, she considered, judging from the horses and fancy carriage. Unless he'd claimed them from some poor loan defaulter. That was even sadder.

"Hungry?" her companion asked, interrupting Sydney's contemplations.

"Famished. I couldn't eat breakfast, I was so nervous, and of course luncheon was out of the question."

Brennan nodded toward the basket at their feet; he still wasn't taking his eyes off the cattle for more than an instant. Sydney eagerly rummaged through the contents, coming up with some cold chicken, but no fork. She shrugged and picked up the drumstick in her hands. "Thank you," she said between bites, earning her a quick half smile.

It was a very pleasant smile, Sydney reflected, remarkably similar to his brother's. Appraising him over the chicken bones, she realized how alike the two really were. Brennan was not quite as handsome as Mr.—no, Lord Mayne. He would do very well, she thought, with a little more attention to his appearance than the simple Belcher necktie and loose-fitting coat he wore. Now that she had the leisure to think back, she recalled that Lord Mayne was dressed bang up to the nines, as Willy would have said. Most likely Brennan couldn't play the dandy because all of his money went to pay gaming debts. She was sorry that an otherwise nice young man should have such a fatal flaw as the gambling fever. Perhaps he only gambled to recoup the family fortune, the same way she did. Sydney smiled in understanding, and wiped her hands on her grimy breeches.

He grinned back. "I've surely never met another young lady like you."

"Of course not, if you only keep low company in gaming hells."

Brennan laughed outright. "I can see you know m'brother better than I thought."

Since he was in such a good mood, Sydney asked if she could drive. Bren almost dropped the reins and needed a few moments to bring the bays back under control. "Then again, maybe you don't know him at all. He'd kill me."

Nodding thoughtfully, Sydney agreed. "Yes, I did note he had a violent nature. I can see where you would be afraid of him."

"Afraid? Of my own brother? You really are an addlepate. They're his cattle, by George. Uh, can you drive?"

"No," Sydney answered happily, "but I've always wanted to try."

On his brother's high-bred pair? Brennan groaned. "You'd better ask Forrest to teach you. Of course," he added lest she get her hopes up, "he's never let a woman take the ribbons yet that I know of." Then again, after Forrest's fantastical behavior today, who could tell?

11

Reunions and Reckonings

"Let me off here, you clunch. I don't want to be seen with you."

"Well, you ain't doing my consequence any good either, I'll have you know." Brennan sniffed disdainfully. "But I have my orders."

"And do you always obey your brother's dictates?" Sydney met him sneer for sneer.

"I do when I'm driving his horses!"

Whatever amity the two had found evaporated when they reached the environs of the city. Brennan's brother had told him to take the chit home, and home he would take her, not set her down like some loose fish halfway across town to make her own way back.

"Don't you think the neighbors might wonder at this fancy rig outside my house and watch to see who is getting out? Let me off at the corner, at least, and I'll run around to the back."

"Now who's being the clunch? I can't just leave the horses standing to see you in, and I ain't leaving till I see you through the door myself. What kind of gentleman do you take me for?"

"None, if you must know. A gentleman would have let me stay at the mill. And a gentleman would not make nasty comments about my appearance, and a gentleman—"

Brennan thought he should do his brother a favor and drown the female while he had the chance, but he had his orders. He kept driving, keeping to side streets and back alleys, until he arrived at the mews behind Mainwaring House. He pulled up before reaching the stable block and told her to get down and wait there. He looked at her suspiciously, then said, "If you think Forrest was angry before, you cannot begin to imagine how he'll be when he gets to Park Lane and you ain't there. He did tell you he was coming, remember?"

Sydney remembered. She waited. She told herself it was only because she didn't know her way around London yet and she was afraid of getting lost.

Bren took the phaeton to the stables and put the bays into the hands of the head groom, who was flummoxed to see the rig and no master, no tiger. "They'll be along presently," was all Bren could think to say, practically running down the mews. "Carry on."

He bundled Sydney into a hackney—at least he didn't have to make any explanations to the driver, no matter how many curious looks they received—and they did not speak until the coach reached the corner near her home. Trying to act as nonchalant as they could considering that they looked like a pair of housebreakers casing the neighborhood, they finally reached Sydney's back door.

"I suppose I should thank you for seeing me home

safely," she said, which sounded rag-mannered even to Sydney, so she grudgingly invited Bren in for refreshment. He was looking peaky after their convoluted journey. She guessed a night creature like Mr. Mainwaring would not take proper care of his health.

Brennan accepted, more out of hope of seeing the scene between his brother and this little hellcat than anything else. Knowing Forrest's opinion of the weaker sex, he thought it might be better than any Drury Lane farce. Because she set a plate of his favorite macaroons in front of him on the kitchen table while she put the tea kettle on, he felt generous. "You just might want to put your skirts on before m'brother gets here," he volunteered. "You do have skirts, don't you?"

"Heavens, you're right. Here," she said, thrusting an oven mitt at him as if he knew what to do with the thing.

"Uh, don't you have any servants, Miss Sydney?" he asked before she could fly away.

"By all that's holy, who did you think was boxing? Their mother is our housekeeper and she's waiting at the inn near Islington. Poor Mrs. Minch will be so worried. I should have gone to her."

"You should have *been* with her, you mean."

"And poor Wally," she went on, ignoring his remark. "Oh, how could I have left?"

"He'll be fine," Brennan reassured her. "Forrest wouldn't let him continue if he wasn't up to snuff. Knowledgeable, don't you know . . . I wonder how long before he gets back?"

Sydney disappeared with a hurried "You stay right here."

* * *

In keeping with the rest of the day, he didn't. When Sydney ran down the stairs, wearing her new jonquil muslin to give her confidence, she heard voices from the front parlor. "Oh, no," she murmured. "What else could go wrong?"

Between Wally getting walloped and a visit from the unpredictably tempered Lord Mayne to look forward to, plenty.

Sydney forced her feet to the parlor door, already knowing what she would see. Sure enough, there was Mr. Mainwaring laughing and chatting, telling the general how honored he was to meet such a great man, and about his hopes to join the army someday. Brennan didn't seem to mind that the general never answered, and Grandfather didn't seem to notice that the young gentleman's eyes never left Winifred. And there was Winnie, sitting demure and rosy-cheeked in the white dimity frock that made her look like an angel, golden curls trailing artlessly down one shoulder. And she, the peagoose, was gazing back at the handsome scamp with that same look of wonder.

Sydney almost searched the little room for blind Cupid and his darts. No, she amended, love wasn't blind. It was stupid and mean. If that wasn't just what Sydney wanted to see, her beautiful sister throwing her cap over the windmill for a ne'er-do-well gamester, the brother of a rake and worse, who did not even have enough blunt to buy himself a commission. She had a vision of delicate Winnie following the drum as the wife of an enlisted man while he gambled away the pittance a private was paid.

Sydney was so upset at the idea, in fact, that when she reached across to take her tea from Winnie, she spilled the cup. On Mr. Mainwaring's legs. "Oh, I am *so* sorry you have to leave us now."

"You're home! Oh, Wally, I'm so happy to see you! Are you all right? Shall I send for a physician? Here's Willy, thank goodness. You don't look so bad. No, don't try to talk. Just give me a hug. And you too, Mrs. Minch. Don't cry, please don't. Wally's safe and Willy's safe and I'm home safe."

They were all in the little kitchen, with Sydney needing to touch each of her friends to reassure herself they were really there. Mrs. Minch was blubbering into the apron she quickly donned, meanwhile putting pots on the stove. Willy held a damp cloth to his jaw, but Wally kept bouncing around the room in boxer's stance.

"You should have seen him, Missy. Why, the big oaf couldn't get his hands up to save himself. Just stood there breathing so hard he nearly sucked up the canvas they put down. Never laid a glove on me after you left, he didn't."

"That's the nicest news I could ever have!" Sydney danced a circuit with him, then made him promise to go rest. "And you, too, Willy. Go find Griff to help you get cleaned up. He'll know what to do and can get the doctor if you need. And don't either of you worry about chores or anything. We'll talk tomorrow."

She gave Wally a final pat, embraced Willy, squeezed what she could of Mrs. Minch's ample form—and walked into the viscount's open arms. She jumped as if she'd just hugged an octopus. "My lord."

"Miss Sydney." He nodded back, grinning. "May I have a moment of your time?"

"Of course, sir. I need to thank you for seeing my people home."

He waved that aside and pointedly stared around the kitchen. Willy was busy at the pump and Mrs. Minch bustled with dinner preparations. "Elsewhere."

"I'm sorry, my lord, but Grandfather is resting now and my sister has gone visiting." There, that should keep her from being alone with him. He was still smiling, but . . .

"I should be honored to meet your family—another time. For now, your own company will suffice."

"But, my lord, I have no other chaperone, and it would not be at all the thing for me to—"

"Flummery, my girl. You cannot claim propriety, not after this day's work. Now, come." He held out his arm and raised his eyebrow. Sydney remembered how he'd lifted her out of the boxing ring as if she weighed no more than a footstool. She didn't doubt he'd resort to such tactics again. Really, the man was a savage. She ignored his arm and led the way to the front parlor, the "company" room. On the way there, however, she decided that she did not need another lecture, especially from him. Especially when he was ruining all of her careful plans. Besides, Grandfather had always said the best defense was a good offense. She put her hands on her hips and turned to face him.

"Before you say one word, my lord, I should like to thank you, and then thank you to get out of my life. My grandfather is ill and he would be terribly upset to think that someone of your type was in the house, or that a wastrel was trifling with my sister. You should know better than to scrape up acquaintance with proper people."

The viscount was astounded. He'd been prepared to be gentle, firm but not overbearing. After all, he'd had the entire afternoon to put a check on his temper. She was only a green girl, he'd rationalized, perhaps she didn't know better. He would just explain the error of her ways, then go about his own business. Somehow his best intentions flew out the window whenever he was near her. Now, when she was looking as appetizing as a bonbon in a stylish yellow frock with a ribbon in her hair, when she didn't smell of attic or stable—now she was back to hurling idiotic insults. He took a deep breath.

"Miss Sydney, I am not a mushroom trying to climb the social ladder; I am not trifling with your sister. Indeed, I have never met the young lady and, if she is anything like you, only pray that I may never do so."

"Not you, you jobbernowl. That wastrel brother of yours was here setting out lures for Winnie, and I won't have it, I tell you! Just being seen with him will ruin her chances!"

"My *brother* could ruin her chances, miss, while it is permissible for you to dress up in boys' clothing? My presence in the house could upset your grandfather, but your presence at a mill couldn't? Do you know what could have happened to you out there today? Some of those men were so foxed, they were beyond manners or morals; some of them never had either to start. How would your ailing grandfather have felt when your raped and ravished body was brought home? You tell me what your precious sister would have done then, Miss High-and-Mighty, if she is too good to associate with a mere second son?"

So much for firm but gentle. Sydney was ashen,

trembling. Forrest felt like the lowest blackguard on earth. He pushed her into a seat and found a decanter on a side table. He sniffed and then poured a tiny amount into one of the glasses. "Here," he offered, putting it into her hand. "I am sorry for speaking so harshly. It's just that I tend to get a little protective of those I feel responsible for. I was concerned for you, that's all."

Sydney stood to her full five feet three inches. Her voice was flat, nearly expressionless when she said, "Yes, I see. I'll go get you the money."

"Money? What does money have to do with anything?"

"The money I owe you. The thousand pounds. I'll just go get it from Willy and then I will not be in your debt and you need not feel responsible for me any longer. I was so excited when they first came home, I forgot all about the winnings."

The viscount poured more brandy into her glass, up to the brim this time, and held it out. "There are no winnings. The bout went five extra rounds and was declared a draw. No winner. No payoff."

Sydney took the glass and drank down the whole thing. Then she coughed and sputtered and turned an odd shade. Seasick green did not look attractive next to the jonquil gown. The viscount pounded her back and shouted at her to breathe, damn it.

"If you kill me," she gasped when she could, "then you'll never get your money back."

"Hang the money, Mischief, it might be worth it anyway." Then he smiled and touched her cheek as lightly as a butterfly's touch. "I'm sorry."

"But it's true, about the money? We didn't win anything?"

"Unless you were clever enough to bet on Wally by the round, or how long he would last."

"Of course not," she answered indignantly. "That would have been disloyal." Then she sighed. "At least we didn't lose any. I can pay you back that part of the sum now anyway."

"Dash it, Sydney, forget about the money. I know it's hard, but try for once to believe me: I am a viscount, not a moneylender."

She finally smiled, showing those dimples that flashed in his dreams. "And I am a lady, but here you've proof that I'm a shameless hoyden. So we are neither what we seem and we are both trying to fool the ton."

Gads, she still did not believe him! A man may as well talk to the wall as reason with a woman! "No matter what you think, I do not need the money."

She was still smiling. "Of course you do. Then you can wash your hands of me and my problems, and I can make sure neither you nor your brother comes near us again." If her goosish sister found Brennan half as attractive as Sydney was finding the viscount, despite knowing his rakehell ways, Winifred was in deep trouble. These Mainwarings were disturbing creatures.

Forrest could feel the heat rising again. He didn't know about Bren, but he did not like being made to feel unwelcome somewhere he hadn't wanted to be in the first place! "Devil take it, will you leave my brother out of this!"

"Of course, if you promise to keep him away from Winnie."

"I'll do my damnedest to warn him away from this lunatic asylum, madam, but I shan't mandate my brother's social life. And let me tell you a few other home truths. I herewith do not care about your reputation. If you do not, why should I? Furthermore, I no longer consider you any kind of responsibility of mine, and I pity the poor man whose concern you do become. His best chance at sanity would be to beat you regularly. And finally, for the last time, I do not want the bloody money!"

Sydney refilled the glass and handed it to him. "You really should not get so excited, you know," she said sweetly. "I believe that's what brought on Grandfather's last seizure. And don't worry, I'll still be able to repay you by the end of the Season."

Forrest took a deep swallow. He should get up and leave, he really should. Better, he should hold that tapestry cushion over her pixie face. Instead he asked, "Just as an observer, mind, not that I intend to get involved, but how do you expect to come into funds? Are you planning another boxing match? Frankly, Mischief, I don't think you have the stomach to watch another, thank goodness."

"No, I won't let Wally take any more challenges. It was his idea, you know. He and Willy have ambitions of their own, to open up an inn if they can just earn enough for the down payment. They're not actually footmen."

"Really? I thought you embraced all your servants."

Even in her naiveté Sydney could recognize his lordship's sarcasm as jealousy. She giggled to think this rogue and rake was jealous of her, Sydney Lattimore, who hadn't even had a come-out Season in town. Then again, maybe she giggled because of the unaccustomed brandy. "Mrs. Minch was my mother's nanny," she explained. "She came to us as housekeeper after Mr. Minch died, so I have known the twins forever, almost like cousins. When I decided to come to London, they wouldn't think of being left behind, so here we all are, trying to better ourselves. Now we'll have to try something else. But don't worry, I have another plan."

The viscount had another drink.

12

Beaux and Bonbons

*W*innie was a Toast. It was official, announced in the *on dit* columns. She was the darling of the *belle monde*. Her beauty was unsurpassed, according to the papers, her manners all that was pleasing. She was sweet and well-spoken, suitably if not grandly connected. The meager dowry was unfortunate, but no matter; she had the most famous footmen in London!

In a few days after the fight, when Willy and Wally were able to accompany the Lattimore sisters on their rounds, they were instantly recognized. What other set of twins was tall, blond, and battered? Aunt Harriet confirmed the fact to a few of her cronies, which meant that all of London knew within hours that the pretty Lattimore chit employed prizefighters as footmen. Instead of redounding to Winnie's discredit, however, as Lady Windham intended, the situation was deemed irregular but not improper by those at the highest ranks of the polite world, some of whose husbands had made a tidy bundle at the match. Winnie was an overnight sensation, especially when she blushingly declined any knowledge of the match.

"Oh, no," she told her admirers, a hint of moisture on her lashes like morning dewdrops. "I . . . I couldn't bear to think of anyone getting hurt, you know, so they did not tell me about it until the next day."

Such tender emotions could only raise her stock with the doyennes of society. Vouchers for Almacks were promised. Winnie's success was guaranteed.

Sydney still preferred walks in the park, making sure she was accompanied by Annemarie, to making those tedious morning visits. She still preferred to stay home with the general, reading and concocting plans, rather than wait endless hours outside another crush just to curtsy to her hostess, dance once or twice with some spotty clothhead Aunt Harriet dragged over to her, then wait another hour for the carriage.

Sydney's position was equivocal at best. She was not formally Out, she was not as beautiful as her sister, she did not have the extensive wardrobe that Winnie did—and she was terrified that she might do or say something to ruin Winnie's chances. So the ton saw her, when they saw her at all, as a shy, retiring sort of girl, content to stay at home.

These days, home was as crowded as the average rout.

Sporting gentlemen came, ostensibly to call on Winnie, but more likely to pass a few minutes with Willy or Wally when they opened the door and took the visitors' hats and gloves. These gents did not much care which twin greeted them—they could not tell the difference anyway—they just wanted to be the first to know if another bout was scheduled. A coin pressed into the footman's hand should guarantee inside knowledge, or a bit of boxing wisdom.

The Tulip set came to Park Lane, at first just to be seen where the fashion was. They came back when they realized what an adornment Miss Lattimore would be on their arms, her golden beauty surely a reflection of their good taste. They wrote odes to her eyebrows and filled the rooms with bouquets, tipping the footman to make sure their offering took precedence.

Military gentlemen arrived in droves to pay their respects to the general's granddaughters. Or to hear a recounting of the match.

The Minch brothers were going to make their down payment one way or another.

With such a wealth of easy pickings, the vultures soon came too: every mama with a marriageable daughter found her way to the Lattimores' teas. The mothers catalogued the gentlemen for future reference; the debs blushed and giggled over the least glimpse of Willy or Wally.

The Dowager Countess Windham was the worst harpy of the lot, in Sydney's estimation. Aunt Harriet made sure Trixie was on view in the Lattimores' parlor every afternoon, displaying the family wealth in gems and laces for all the eligibles, and just in case Lord Mayne came to call. Everyone knew of his extraordinary affiliation with the footmen at Islington; they were waiting to see if the elusive viscount expanded the association here in London.

How should she know? Winifred asked in confusion when pumped for information by Aunt Harriet. She never met the man. He was most likely just another eccentric they were better off not knowing, Sydney added, firmly believing her own words.

The viscount did not call, neither did his brother. "I don't understand," Winnie fretted. "He said he would call the next day."

Sydney understood perfectly. She'd ordered the general's man Griffith, standing in for the footmen right after the fight, to deny Lord Mainwaring the house. By the time Wally and Willy were back tending the door, Sydney had turned her sister's mind against the good-looking makebait.

"He most likely heard about your tiny dowry. A man like that cannot afford a poor wife, so he wouldn't waste his time."

"Do . . . do you mean he's a fortune hunter?" Winnie clutched a tiny scrap of lace to her cheek. "I knew he was a second son, but . . ." Sarah Siddons could not have portrayed Virtue Distressed better.

"I have it on the best of authorities"—his own brother, though she wouldn't tell Winnie—"that his character is unsteady. I know for a fact that his closest associates are of low morals. And," she intoned, "there is gambling." As in leprosy. "Think of the hand-to-mouth existence his unfortunate wife would lead, after he went through all of her money, of course."

"Oh, the poor thing," Winnie wept. The next time Lord Brennan Mainwaring did call, he was cheerfully admitted by Willy, who would have done anything for Lord Mayne or his younger brother. Winnie turned her back on him and let some fop in yellow Cossack trousers read a poem to her rosebud lips. Brennan left, and did not come back.

There was one other worry furrowing Winnie's

brow, to Sydney's horror. "Stop that, you'll make wrinkles! Worrying is my job!"

"But Lord Scoville doesn't like all the attention we're getting, Sydney. He doesn't think it's proper."

"Oh, pooh, he just wants you all to himself. Besides, there will be something else to steal the public eye next week. Some debutante will run off with a junior officer, or some basket-scrambler will lose his fortune at the baize tables. As long as our names aren't mentioned in either instance," she warned, not so subtly, "Scoville will get over his pet."

"He thinks we should dismiss the twins."

"Why, that prosy, top-lofty bore. How dare he— that is, I'm sure he didn't realize we consider the Minches as family."

"Oh, yes, he did. He doesn't think that's proper either. 'Ladies should not become overfamiliar with the servants,' he says."

Sydney hoped the pompous windbag became overfamiliar with Willy's fist one day, but for now he was their best paddle to row them out of River Tick.

Everyone in London seemed to know the way to their door, including a past visitor to Little Dedham. Mrs. Ott was not actually an acquaintance, being more a relation to the vicar's wife's dead brother, who used to visit there. The girls must have been too young then, but Mrs. Ott recalled meeting the general once or twice. If the general recalled the rather plump woman in darkest crepe, he did not say.

Mrs. Ott was calling, she told Sydney, because Mrs. Vicar Asquith had written that her dear friends were coming to town, and could Bella help make them feel more at home. So there she was, bringing a plum cake, just like folks did in the country.

Sydney would have been suspicious of anyone trying to scrape up a connection like that, but Mrs. Ott did not seem to want anything more from the family than their friendship. She had no daughter to marry off, no son to introduce. She did not wish introductions or invitations, for she went out seldom, still being in mourning.

"Dear Lady Bedford keeps urging me to attend one of her dos, but I cannot enjoy myself knowing my dear Major Ott is no longer with me." Mrs. Ott had to stifle a sob in her handkerchief. "I am a poor army widow like your dear mama," she told Sydney with another sniffle for the departed. "That is, I ain't poor. My husband had other income than his regular pay." Paddy O'Toole certainly had.

So Sydney welcomed the quaint grieving widow even if she could not quite recall Mrs. Asquith's mention of a relation in London, and Mrs. Ott's speech was broader than she was used to. But those were country manners, she excused, and they were not altogether unwelcome after the starchy *grandes dames* of London. Besides, the plum cake was delicious.

"Oh, that's just a hobby of mine, don't you know. For when Mon-shure Pierre has his half days off. Here, try another piece, dearie, and why don't you call me Bella? I can tell we're going to be friends. You just call on me whenever you need anything."

"Do you like to read, Mrs. Ott?" Sydney asked. "The reason I inquire is that my sister is really not interested, and I should like to visit the lending libraries more. I wouldn't think of going by myself, but my sister often needs our abigail, and I hate to take the household staff away from their tasks. I

117

thought that perhaps if you were ever going, that is, if you do not think I am too forward . . ."

"Not at all, dearie, not at all. Why, I said you could count on old Bella Bu—Ott for anything. And I love to read. Ain't that a coincidence? It's my favorite thing, right after cooking. Lawks-a-mercy, I haven't had a good read since I don't know when. Why don't we go right now? I have the carriage outside, with m'driver and footman."

"Oh, no, I couldn't impose," Sydney said, but she was glad to be refuted. She was delighted that this new colleague not only shared her interests but could quiet Aunt Harriet's carping about a chaperone. A respectable older widow with servants and all ought to satisfy the strictest notions of propriety. Even the outré Lord Mayne would be satisfied that her reputation was well protected.

The servants weren't quite what Sydney would have selected for a genteel household.

"Just ignore 'em," Bella advised as she saw Sydney pause at the doorstep. "I try to. You might say my husband left them to me. Their names are Chessman and Rand, but I call 'em Cheeseface and Rarebit. You can see why."

Chessman held the carriage door. Actually he hid behind the carriage door and Bella had to shout to him to close it once they were inside. He had a powdered wig and a lead-whitened face, and his livery had a large sash around his thin middle. (The undertaker reported that the dead footman had been caught in his master's bedroom.)

The coachman did have rabbity teeth hanging over his lower lip; otherwise he was bundled head to toe in coat, boots, cape, hat, and muffler. Sydney could not even tell what color hair the man had, and he was so small she wondered if he had the strength to manage the horses. Oh, well, she thought, they were going only a few blocks.

Actually, they were going to Bella's house in Chelsea. Since Sydney had not been condemned in the ton for her part in the prizefight—and the Ottos never knew how big her part was—and Lord Scoville seemed to be cooling off toward the sister, Bella'd had the knacky notion of kidnapping the chit. Everyone knew Mayne stood by her servants through the boxing match; he was certain to ransom the gel.

"I ain't going to hire no witness to drive the coach," Bella said, "so which of you is going to do it, the runt or the milksop?"

The milksop won, the runt drove . . . for the first time in fifteen years, and badly. In a few blocks of the lending library, Randy scraped the side of a standing carriage, ran over a small delivery wagon, and wrapped one of the wheels around a lamppost. Sydney suggested they get out and walk. There was nothing for it but to acquiesce, so Bella got down and informed the driver that she would take a hackney home, dear boy, not to worry. As soon as Sydney's back was turned, Bella buried her reticule about an inch deep in Randy's scalp.

"Coming, dear," she called, grabbing Chester's sleeve before he could shab off, now that the day's plan was abandoned. "And you better stick like glue, pudding-heart," she spat at him. "Someone's got to pick out my damn books."

The trip could not be counted a success by anyone, especially Bella Bumpers Ott. If Sydney thought her new friend a trifle odd, Bella's reading tastes confirmed the supposition. Sydney found Miss

Austen's latest work and her favorite Scott ballads while Mrs. Ott checked out *A Gentleman's Guide to Rome* and *Statistical Configurations of Probabilities.* And Sydney would rather spend the rest of her days inside the house than put one foot inside the carriage again.

The next time Mrs. Ott called, with a poppy seed cake and an invitation to visit the Tower, Sydney refused, though she would dearly have liked to go. Winifred never wanted to accompany her; she feared the place would give her nightmares.

Trying to salve Mrs. Ott's feelings, for she could see the older woman was screwing her face up to cry, Sydney offered a box of chocolates, each piece wrapped in silver paper. "Please, ma'am, will you do me the favor of tasting one of these candies? I ask because you are such a fine cook, and I value your judgment. You see, this is an old recipe from Little Dedham. The church ladies make them for Twelfth Night. Perhaps you've had them before? No? How strange. Anyway, my housekeeper and her sons are thinking of going into the confectionery business, and I thought I would help them along by soliciting an expert opinion. Not that I intend to have anything to do with the sales, of course."

Of course. Sydney had the profit margin figured to the ha'penny, a list of every sweet shop in London and the outskirts, a plan to promote them through the ton, and a schedule whereby she and the Minches could produce enough bonbons and still see Winifred through the Season.

"Delicious," Mrs. Ott pronounced. "What's that in the center, eh? Blackberry cordial, you say? Clever, but I think it could use a drop more, maybe a smidgen of rum. Do you think your friends would accept my help? I love to putter in the kitchen, and I *do* like to see the lower orders improve themselves."

The next few days were busy ones, experimenting and tasting. Sydney fell into bed each night, more exhausted than she would have thought, but at least she no longer dreamed of blue eyes that raged like a wild sea and smiled like a placid lake.

The general's man, Griffith, was the designated sales force. The Minch brothers were too recognizable; no one must suspect the Lattimores were in trade. Griff brought free samples to some of the shops and chatted with the proprietors while they tasted. He, too, couldn't wait to reach his pallet.

Sworn to secrecy, Trixie took some home to Lady Windham, who declared she hadn't had such a good night's rest in years, and ordered a dozen boxes from her favorite tart shop to give to her friends.

In no time at all Sydney was up to her dimples in orders. Mrs. Ott mixed the rum-flavored chocolate. Willy and Wally poured the heavy vats into molds. Mrs. Minch filled the centers with the blackberry cordial syrup. Sydney and Trixie wrapped each piece in its silver twist. Winifred lettered signs to go with each package: CHURCHLADIES' CORDIAL COMFITS AND COMPOSERS. Griff delivered the boxes. Sydney did the books. She figured they would start to see a profit over the initial outlay for materials in a week or two.

The candies kept selling, the money kept coming in, and Bella kept pouring more and more laudanum into the vats.

13

The Marriage Mart

"What do you mean, I have to go to Almacks? The match was a draw, remember? All bets were off."

Forrest admired the high shine on his Hessians. "Didn't you drive my bays?"

"But, but, you asked me to!" Bren sputtered.

"And now I am asking you to go to Almacks. Think how happy the duchess will be. Furthermore, they are saying in the clubs that Miss Lattimore will be making her debut appearance there tonight. Surely that's incentive enough to suffer knee smalls for one evening."

Bren wore a long face. "She don't like me. She ain't even home most of the time, at least not to me. When she is, she's sighing over some drooling mooncalf and his mawky rhymes. I thought we were getting along fine at first."

"So I deduced," the viscount replied dryly, having been forced to sit through his brother's rhapsodies on Miss Lattimore's infinite charms. Bren had not *quite* drooled. "I see Miss Sydney's fine hand at work there. She wants better for her sister."

"I suppose you mean Scoville," Bren conceded disconsolately.

"Not just that. I, ah, may have mentioned to Miss Sydney your difficulties with those gambling debts." He held up his hand to still Bren's protests. "I didn't know I'd ever see her again, or that she'd take my ill-advised words so much to heart. I'm afraid Miss Sydney thinks you are a hardened gamester." Forrest wasn't about to tell his brother what she thought of himself!

"But it was only that one time! Well, maybe a time or two before, but that coil wasn't my fault. I've hardly wagered since!"

"Try convincing Miss Sydney of that." Forrest's cynicism came from long experience.

"Well, she don't think much of you either."

"Miss Sydney's mind is particularly tenacious. She's a difficult female to reason with. In fact," he went on with a frown of reminiscence, "she's a difficult female altogether. Nevertheless, it is also her first time at Almacks, and I would appreciate your making her feel comfortable."

"She's more like to spill the punch bowl over my head. If you care so much, why don't you go do the pretty with the girl?"

Forrest grimaced. "Can you imagine what would happen if I had even one dance with her? The gossipmongers would have the banns read! That's why I haven't called in Park Lane myself."

"And I'm not quite the social lion, so it's fine to sacrifice me, right? Hang it, Forrest, the chit's got less sense than a carp. She's just as liable to tie her garters in public or wear the general's uniform."

"Or dance with the servants. That's why I want you to go and look after her."

Brennan considered his options, then nodded. "I bet she dances like an angel."

"Mischief? I mean Sydney?" Forrest briefly imagined the heaven of having her in his arms.

"No, Miss Winifred Lattimore. I'd be surprised if your scapegrace even knows how to dance. Well, I think I'll toddle over to Park Lane this morning and see if Miss Winifred will speak to me. If she'll give me a dance or two, I'll go. Otherwise, bro, you'll just have to face the music yourself. Literally."

The man Griffith turned Bren away at the door with a surly "The ladies are not at home this morning." Having come this long way, Bren decided to step around back to the kitchen—he knew the way well enough—and check on Wally and Willy.

The place looked like some mad scientist's laboratory. A large order had come just this morning, of all days, when they needed to get ready for Almacks! The girls were so sleepy, Mrs. Minch insisted they all had to rest that afternoon so they would be at the top of their form for the big evening. Even Sydney was ordered to nap.

Sydney had not wanted to go, naturally, to face another evening of sitting in little gilt chairs along the wall, pretending she didn't care. The assembly also promised a gathering of society's most exacting hostesses. One foot wrong and a girl might as well join a nunnery. Sydney was so tired she couldn't possibly remember all the rules Aunt Harriet had been drumming into her head. For once Sydney and her aunt agreed on something: the fear that Sydney would land them all in the briars. Lady Windham decreed, however, that the Almacks patronesses would take Sydney's refusal as a personal affront.

"So you'll attend, girl. You'll sit still and keep your mouth shut. You'll wear white like every other debutante and you won't complain about the music or the refreshments or the partners found for you."

Now, that was an evening to look forward to! First Sydney had to rush them through this latest order, if they had enough boxes and Trixie didn't eat all the profits, claiming she was just checking to ensure consistent quality. Everyone else was working double time, and thank goodness for Mrs. Ott, who was keeping those vats of chocolate coming. One more batch and they could all—

"Oh, no, not you! Get out! Don't look!" Sydney shouted. Mrs. Minch tried to hide the molds with her wide body, and Winifred turned as white as the huge apron she wore. Trixie giggled.

"Too late, brat," Lord Mainwaring announced, stepping farther into the kitchen. "If you didn't want anyone to see, you should have kept the door closed. 'Sides, I didn't cry rope on you over the Islington fiasco, so you should know I'll keep mum. It looks like fun. Can I help?"

He was right, it was too late. Winifred was already offering him a candy and showing him her neatly lettered signs.

"Perfection!" he declared, and everyone but Sydney cheered. She wasn't sure if he meant the bonbon or Winnie. "And if they are good for the nerves," he went on, "I'll send some home to my mother, who could certainly use a composer. She'll tell her friends and you'll have a whole new mar-

125

ket." Then he happily took his place next to Trixie, wrapping the candies in their silver paper.

Trixie licked her fingers and giggled again. She was giddy with Mrs. Ott's whispered suggestion that she take some boxes into Almacks, where the food was so scarce; she was thrilled to be doing something her mother would hate; she was in alt at sitting beside Lord Mainwaring. She was drunk.

Almacks was supposed to be dull, but this was absurd! Everyone sat around yawning. Aunt Harriet was dozing in a corner with some of her friends, leaving her daughter Sophy, Lady Royce, to watch out for the younger ladies. Sophy had long decided that her status as a young matron entitled her to a degree of license unknown while she was under her mama's thumb. She further considered her freedoms doubled since her husband was abroad with the Foreign Office. Tonight she was more concerned with disappearing to the balcony with hard-eyed older gentlemen than in finding partners for her sister Beatrix or her cousin Sydney. Winifred's card, as a matter of course, was filled within minutes of their entry to the hallowed rooms on King Street.

Lady Royce was too busy pursuing her latest dalliance to stop Trixie from accepting a waltz without permission from one of the patronesses, but no matter. The lady patronesses were just as logy and disinterested in platter-faced chits as Aunt Harriet. Her good friend Lady Drummond-Burrell was actually snoring. Without the doyennes and dowagers pushing them to their duty, the younger men formed groups of their own on the sidelines or in the refreshments room, discussing the latest curricle race to Bath.

So Sydney sat in her white dress until Winnie brought over one or another of her surplus coxcombs, or some young buck took the chance she might know something about boxing. Sydney fervently declared it the most barbaric sport imaginable, which ended those conversations fairly quickly.

Now that her dragon of a mama wasn't guarding her, every gentleman with pockets to let asked Trixie to dance. She went off gaily, more often to the refreshments room than to the dance floor, leaving Sydney alone and uncomfortable. By the time the doors closed at eleven o'clock, though, Trixie hardly knew her name, much less the figures of the quadrille. Proper manners forced the fortune hunters to ask Sydney to dance in default, to no one's benefit or pleasure.

Trixie's doughy complexion was taking on a grayish cast, and she kept trying to rest her head on Sydney's shoulder. Embarrassed and concerned, Sydney tried to catch Sophy's eye. They may as well go home anyway, for all the notice Lady Jersey, et al., were taking of them. Contrarily, Lady Royce was finding the place unusually stimulating. She sent one of her cicisbei off to fetch a restorative lemonade for Trixie and chided Sydney for not being more accommodating.

"Why, you were positively snappish to Lord Dunne, and he's worth ten thousand a year."

"Not to me, he's not," Sydney replied, "not when he keeps squeezing my hand in that oily way of his. And I truly do have the headache, Sophy. Can't we go— Good heavens, what's he doing here?"

All eyes—all that were open anyway—were turned to the door. Standing framed by candlelight in the hush between dances was Lord Mayne, magnificent in black and white evening formals. The only dash of color from his curly black hair to his shiny black pumps was a blue sapphire in his perfect cravat. His blue eyes would be gleaming to match, Sydney knew, though she could not see from so far away.

He looked like a true nonesuch, but she knew better. Sydney's opinion of this supposedly exclusive club fell another notch. "You mean they let in people like him?" she asked in disgust.

Trixie drawled back, "La, you silly cabbage, Almacks *exists* for people like him."

She was right. All the languorous mamas pushed their daughters forward; the torpid patronesses bestirred themselves to have their hands kissed; matrons like Sophy, not the least bit sleepy, tugged down the necklines of their gowns and licked their lips.

Sheep, Sydney thought, they were all sheep. The ninnyhammers thought that since he had a title and a pleasant face—all right, a heart-stoppingly handsome face—then he must be worth knowing. Hah! You could dress your cat up in a lace bib and sit him at the table; he would still put his face in the food. Just look at Lord Mayne smiling at those boring old dowagers, when she knew what little patience the foul-tempered peer had. Look at him making his bows to several giggly young chits, when she knew the rake could send them fleeing to their mothers' skirts with an improper suggestion. And look at him kissing Cousin Sophy's hand! Why, that—

"Lady Royce, how charmingly you look tonight. No, I should say how particularly lovely, for you are always in looks." Sophy tapped his arm with her fan and pushed her chest out. If she took another deep breath, Sydney seethed, Almacks would truly be enlivened. Then he turned to Sydney and bowed. She gritted her teeth and curtsied, almost low enough for royalty, just out of spite. She could behave like a lady, so there.

Sophy's fan hit the floor. "You mean you actually know the chit? I mean, the gossip and rumors and all, but I never dreamed . . . Why, Sydney, you sly thing."

Lord Mayne smoothly interrupted: "We've never been formally introduced, actually. I was hoping you could do the honors. You see," he went on, not exactly lying, "my mother asked me to look up the daughters of an old friend of hers." Sydney noted that the silver-tongued devil did not mention what old friend.

Sophy performed her part before reluctantly leaving on the arm of her next partner. A fine chaperone she was, Sydney stewed, leaving an unfledged deb alone with a shifty character who was grinning at her discomfort, blast him. And everyone else was staring! She tried to kick Trixie into escort duty, but the caperwit actually winked at the viscount before putting her head down on Sydney's seat. He raised an eyebrow.

"She was, ah, tired out from all the dancing."

Forrest raised his quizzing glass and surveyed the room in what Sydney considered a horribly foppish manner. "There seems to be a great deal of that going around."

"I always understood Almacks to be quite staid.

I can't imagine what would bring a man like you here."

"Can't you, Mischief?" he asked with that lopsided smile. Sydney looked around to make sure no one heard him. "I came to dance with your sister."

For a moment she felt her heart sink to her slippers, then outrage took over. "Well, I wish you wouldn't. You'll ruin everything! I imagine one dance with you would label her fast. Lord Scoville would have a kittenfit if he saw her in such company."

"Is that really what you think, Mischief?" He flipped open a cloisonné box and took a pinch of snuff, one-handedly.

No, she really thought Winifred would fall in love with the rake and follow his blandishments right down the garden path! Out loud she said, "Don't call me that," forcing herself not to stamp her foot. "And you need not persist in these dandified affectations for my sake. You might humbug the ton, but I know you for what you are, and I do not want you near my sister."

"I am continually amazed at what you know and what you don't. Nevertheless, my dear, I am going to have the next dance with her. My brother was promised a set with Miss Lattimore, but fell too ill to attend. He was devastated that she might take umbrage at his defection, so I gave my word to deliver his regrets. I always keep my word. Like now, I'll promise not to eat the gel if you'll stop scowling for all the *haute monde* to see. After all, I do have *my* reputation to consider."

Sydney smiled, although she was even more worried for Winnie if he was going to be charming. "I hope nothing serious ails Lord Mainwaring. He seemed fine this morning."

Lord Mayne was watching the dancers, a slight frown on his face. "No, something about overindulging in a box of candies he purchased for our mother. Some new chocolates that were all the crack, he said, and my other mission was to have another box sent on to Sussex for the duchess."

"Did he, ah, say anything else about them? Where he got them, perhaps?" Sydney bit her lip.

"No, but most confectioners seem to carry them suddenly. I even thought I recognized a box or two in the refreshments room here, if you'd like to try one."

"No, I, ah, have a few in my reticule, as a matter of fact. I was told they served only stale cake, you see." Sydney looked at Trixie slumped in her chair, snoring. Aunt Harriet and her friends were in no better frame, the ones who hadn't already left on the arms of their footmen. Sophy was now doing the stately Galliard as if it were a galop. And she herself had the headache. "Did you say Lord Mainwaring got sick from them?"

"I can't be sure. He couldn't wake up enough to describe the symptoms. I had to leave him in the hands of my father's valet before they closed the doors here. Perhaps I'll taste one of these new sensations after my dance with your sister."

"Please do. I'd like to hear your opinion." Her headache was getting worse every second.

14

Waltzes and Woes

"*We* talked about his mother," Sydney said for about the hundredth time. One would think the man some kind of oracle the way the other girls on the sidelines wanted to know his every word. "No, I was only introduced to him tonight and, yes, I do think Lord Mayne and Winifred make an attractive couple."

Lord Mayne and Sally Jersey also made an attractive couple, as did Lord Mayne and Lady Delverson, Lord Mayne and Lady Stanhope, Lord Mayne and Miss Beckwith. Sydney finally escaped to the ladies' withdrawing room, sick and tired of hearing the wretch's name on everyone's lips. Which reminded her that she was also sick and tired. The chocolates!

She hurried to the refreshments room, which was nearly deserted now. Sydney had no doubt everyone stayed in the dancing area to watch Lord Mayne. The gentlemen were wagering on his next partner or trying to figure out the new arrangement of his neckcloth. The ladies were hoping to be that next partner, or admiring his graceful leg. Prinny himself wouldn't have drawn more attention from the gudgeons. Sydney had more important matters to consider.

Drat Trixie! She said she was taking some boxes to her mother in lieu of stopping at a sweetshop for them, but here they were. Sydney counted three empty boxes and another half filled, hidden behind a fern. She stuffed candies into her reticule until it looked as if she had a small cannonball in it, then dug around in the fern, burying the rest. That's where he found her.

He looked at her dirty glove through his quizzing glass and muttered something suspiciously like, "I knew I shouldn't have taken my eyes off you for a minute." Sydney blushed and felt her face grow even hotter when he asked, "You do not dance, *petite*?"

She was not about to admit that no one asked her. Then the strains of the next number started and she could thankfully claim, "It's a waltz, my lord. I have not been given permission."

"Then perhaps you'll take a turn about the room with me," he offered, placing her hand in the crook of his elbow.

Sydney couldn't refuse without making a scene, for a flock of gawkers had followed him to the refreshments room. She could see tongues wagging everywhere. She wanted to ask him why he was doing this thing, making a byword of her, but there were too many interruptions. Gentlemen kept shaking his hand, telling him how glad they were to see him in town and inviting him for dinner, cards, morning rides. Ladies of all ages nodded and smiled and batted their eyelashes at him, while the prominent hostesses begged him to attend their next affairs. Or *affaires*, Sydney thought maliciously. Finally she blurted out, "They like you."

He stopped walking and looked around. "I never thought about it in those terms. I have known many of these people my entire life and value their respect. I hold some in affection, and believe my regard is returned. I don't see a single soul here whom I have wronged, so yes, I suppose you could say they like me."

"But, but why? I mean, how could they when you—"

He laughed. "Ah, Mischief, your candor delights me. Much more so than your buffle-headed reasoning." He patted her arm on his and started walking again. "They like me," he told her, "because I really am a fine fellow. Honest, polite, helpful, eventempered." He lightly tapped her fingers with his quizzing glass when she started to giggle. "I know everybody and treat them equally, no matter rank or fortune; I try not to abuse the privileges my title and wealth give me."

Sydney was giggling even harder. "O ye of little faith," he chided, mock-frowning at the gamin grin she gave him. "You doubt my power? What if I said I could bring you into fashion with just one dance?"

Sydney laughed. "Gammon, my lord, no one could do that."

"Just watch, and keep smiling."

He was gone a few moments, only till the end of the set. When the music next began, he returned, bowed, and held his arms out to her, his blue eyes dancing with deviltry.

134

Sydney looked around uncertainly. It seemed all eyes in the place were on her. "But . . ."

"Chin up, little one. Didn't your grandfather tell you that good soldiers never back down under fire?"

"But it's a waltz." She looked over to where the patronesses stood, the ones who were lively enough to stand. Lady Jersey nodded and waved her hand.

"Sally likes me," was his simple comment.

"But they just played a waltz."

"The orchestra likes me." He dropped his hands. "You do know how to waltz, don't you?"

She nodded. "I practiced with the twins."

He laughed that Brennan was right: Mischief did dance with the servants. Then he swept her onto the floor the way no cousinly footman ever had.

Sydney's head was spinning. It must be the headache coming back, she decided, but she no longer felt the least bit tired. Her feet were as light as soap bubbles, and her hand where he clasped it tingled as if from cold. But she wasn't cold, not at all. He smiled down at her and she could only gaze back, her eyes drawn to his like magnets, and she smiled. Her heart was beating in waltz tempo and her thoughts were swirling like clouds in a kaleidoscope. Heavens, what had they put in those chocolates?

She realized the dance was over when Lord Mayne raised her hand and, turning it over, kissed her wrist. Of course, she thought, her fingers were dirty. He winked and said, "Now watch."

One gentleman after another asked to put his name on her dance card. They tripped over each other to fetch her lemonade. And these were not callow youths who were busy digging in all the ferns, at any rate. They were Mayne's friends and contemporaries, men of means and influence and taste—just like him, she was forced to concede. These gentlemen spoke of books and politics and her grandfather's renowned career. They were interesting and interested in her, and did not seem to mind when she gave her own opinions about anything and everything. She felt more alive than she had in days.

Sydney tried to rouse Trixie between sets, but her cousin only stirred enough to visit the room set aside for the ladies, where she had earlier stashed the other three boxes of Churchladies' Cordial Comfits. Sydney was too busy enjoying her new popularity to notice Trixie passing the treats around to her girlfriends and bringing a box over to her mother. Lady Windham was staring confusedly in Sydney's direction, wondering if her two nieces had changed identities.

A few dances later, *he* was back, piercing Sydney's euphoria with a dagger look. "It is time to go home, Miss Sydney" was all he said through his clenched jaw. He took her arm, none too gently, when she protested that it was early yet and she was having the best time ever, thanks to him. "There will be other balls," he ground out, then added, "with any luck."

Lord Mayne stuffed Lady Windham and her daughters into their carriage. Trixie offered him a chocolate while Lady Windham and Sophy tittered over his well-filled stockings. He tossed the candy to the ground in disgust and ordered the driver to move on.

Sydney was content that she and Winnie were to travel in Lord Mayne's more elegant coach, until he followed them into the carriage. She supposed he was going to spoil everything now with his thundercloud expression, just to prove he could do that too. She stared out the window, not talking.

Winifred was used to her sister's sitting mumchance in company and knew it was her responsibility to fill the silence with polite conversation. She tried. "Did I thank you for the dance, my lord?"

"Twice."

"Ah, did I ask you to send my sympathy to Lord Mainwaring?"

"At least that many times."

"And to thank your mother for her interest?"

"Yes."

"Then could you stop the carriage, my lord," she asked in that same sweet tone. "I think I am going to be sick."

"Whatever made you cockleheads think you could cook, much less measure?" Lord Mayne was shouting. Sydney sat at the kitchen table, miserably huddled over her third cup of black coffee. Forrest was waiting with the fourth, and she didn't even like coffee. Winifred was suffering in the hands of their abigail, but Sydney was not going to be permitted such an easy death.

"You are the most blithering idiot it's ever been my misfortune to meet." His lordship was in full spate. "It wasn't enough for you to threaten your whole family with scandal by going into trade, not you! You had to try to poison the whole ton! And at Almacks of all places!"

Sydney did not blame Trixie for that particular lunacy; she knew the girl was jingle-brained and should have watched her. It was all her fault. She just sat, feeling more blue-deviled.

Wally tried to exonerate them. "We didn't set out to poison anyone. It must have been a bad batch."

"And I suppose you didn't sample every one?" He could tell by the guilty looks and mottled complexions that they had. He poured the twins more coffee. "Damn if you two haven't taken too many punches to the head! And you, miss, should have been left out at birth for the wolves."

"I was," she sniffed through gathering tears. "The wolves threw me back." Then she was crying in earnest. "Do you think . . . that is, will they send me to jail?"

Forrest cursed and handed her his handkerchief. "Coventry maybe, brat, not jail. Who exactly knows that you were responsible?"

"Everyone in the house except Grandfather and—"

Willy shook his head. "The general enjoyed the bonbons so well, I told him we made 'em. He won't talk."

"—And Annemarie."

Wally shook *his* head. "She kept smelling the chocolate, so I showed her the molds. But she's sweet on me. She won't peach on us."

Forrest was tearing his hands through his hair. "Who else?"

"Trixie, but she can't say anything. She's the one who brought them to Almacks. And even if she tells her mama, Aunt Harriet cannot tell, for she handed them around to all her friends."

"Anyone else?"

Sydney started to weep again. Through the folds of the viscount's handkerchief she whimpered, "An old friend from home . . . and your brother was here this morning, helping."

There was a moment of silence. Sydney began to

think she might live through the night. Then she had to grab for the coffee cup as his fist came down on the table, rattling the china. "Well, I told you to keep him away," Sydney cried into the cloth.

"To protect your sister's reputation, fiend seize it, not his! You didn't warn me you'd involve him in your hen-witted schemes, or try to kill him with your concoctions! I should have shipped him to the front lines. He'd be safer."

"I'm sorry," she said, "and you can be sure that I won't mention his name if they bring me in front of the assizes. And I promise not to tell them that you lent me the money to start the business."

"Hell and damnation!" Then he took a look at Sydney, so woebegone, so wretched, her hazel eyes swimming in tears, and his anger melted. "Don't worry, Mischief, I'll try to fix it."

She brightened immediately. "Oh, can you? I'll be in your debt forever. How silly, I'm already in your debt. But what shall you do?"

The viscount sighed and got up to leave. "Forget about the damned money, Mischief, and go to bed."

She followed him to the door. "But maybe I can help."

"That's the last thing I need," he teased, just to see her dimples. Then he wiped a tear away from her cheek with his finger. "I'll see you in the morning. Wear that pretty yellow dress."

Embarrassed, she twitched at the folds of her white lace gown. "I know it's not becoming on me, but Aunt Harriet said I had to wear white."

"And you always follow Aunt Harriet's rules?"

She chuckled and answered, "Only when I am playing her game."

There was nothing Forrest could do that night, beyond shooting his own brother, that is. And he was too restless for bed, disturbed more than he ever wanted to be by Sydney's unhappiness. Her eyes should never be dimmed with woe; they should have stars in them, as they had when she looked up at him during the waltz. Her mouth was never meant for drooping sorrow; those full lips were meant for laughing, or kissing. And her body—

He went to visit his current mistress.

Forrest did not own the little house in Kensington, but he was presently paying the rent, so he let himself in despite the near darkness of the place. Lighting a candle, he found his way to Ava's bedchamber. There she lay, fast asleep, propped up on a mound of frothy pillows. Her filmy negligee was open invitingly, but her mouth was open too, trailing a thread of drool and issuing raspy snores. An open box of bonbons, each wrapped in silver paper, rested by her side.

The viscount shrugged. He wasn't in the mood anyway. He wrote a check and left it on the dresser. She would find it in the morning and know he wasn't coming back. Forrest left, feeling relieved, and not just because she hadn't fallen asleep while he was making love to her.

15

Double Trouble

*M*orning came too early. Sydney groaned and went back to bed. Minutes later, it seemed, Annemarie was shaking her awake. Certain the authorities must have come for her, Sydney hid under the bedclothes. "No, I won't go!"

"But, mademoiselle, the handsome *vicomte* waits downstairs."

"That's even worse." Sydney burrowed deeper.

Forrest had been up before daybreak, buying all the unsold boxes of comfits in the stores. He made sure the shopkeepers believed the supply was for a personage of the highest rank. This unidentified gentleman with the large sweet tooth was also hiring the confection's creator, so there would be no more of the candies forthcoming. And no diplomatic way of complaining about their ingredients.

He drove the carriageload of boxes to the naval hospital, where a doctor friend of his gladly accepted the donation. A heavy hand with rum and laudanum would not come amiss there.

Then Forrest went to the park, greeted several friends, and listened to gossip of foxed females at the bastion of propriety, Almacks. He even added a rumor of his own, wondering if some young blades had poured Blue Ruin into the punch bowl. If the Lattimores' names were mentioned at all, it was with a partial compliment, such as "Lovely girls, aren't they?" Such hesitancy he correctly interpreted as an inquiry to his own interest in the sisters. He carefully showed very little. "Quite charming if you like sweet schoolroom misses. Connection of my mother's, don't you know?"

He repeated his taradiddles in the clubs, convincing everyone that his relationship was the most casual, so the Lattimores were fair game. Of course the girls were not to be trifled with, it was understood, without incurring the Duchess of Mayne's disfavor, which indubitably meant facing the viscount.

Satisfied with the morning's work and wondering if he had ever told so many lies before, his lordship went to Park Lane. Sydney was anything but a sweet schoolgirl, and he almost regretted bringing her to the attention of the more observant members of the ton. But how could anyone have swallowed that Banbury tale? he wondered. Forrest thought of Mischief as a freckled moppet in red-gold pigtails doing her sums on a slate, and chuckled. She was most likely figuring percentage points from the cradle! She didn't even have a schoolgirl's shape, but he had lost enough sleep thinking of her rounded figure in his arms. Ah, well, he told himself, her feet were firmly planted in the marriage market now, and it was better that way. He could go home to Sussex with a clear conscience as soon as he delivered his messages.

"The young ladies are still abed," Willy—or Wally—told him.

"Get her" was all Forrest said. He didn't have to specify which sister he wished to see, nor that he dashed well would go fetch her himself if he had to.

Forrest chatted with the general about the war news while he waited. This was more satisfying than such conversations tended to be with his own father, who threw newspapers around whenever anyone disagreed with him. The general merely pounded his armchair a few times.

Then Sydney arrived, dressed in a peach-colored round gown that highlighted the warm tones of her skin. He wasn't surprised that she didn't wear the yellow gown, in defiance of his wishes, nor that she sat on the stool near her grandfather's feet, as if for protection. He wasn't even surprised at how heavy-eyed and tousled she looked, only at his body's reaction to seeing her like a woman who had just been made love to. A schoolgirl, hah!

Griffith came and wheeled the general away, over Sydney's protests. Forrest smiled and jingled some coins in his pocket. Griff liked him too.

"I'm sorry I cannot stay and visit with you, my lord, but I have to see Mrs. Minch about the day's menus."

"I'm sure whatever she selects will be fine, as long as you don't have a hand in the cooking. Don't you want to hear how your adventure turned out?"

"I already know; I haven't been arrested yet." She waved her hand around at the flowers on the buhl table, on the mantel, in the hall. "Some of them are even for me, according to Annemarie, so we're not even to be ostracized. And no, I do not want another lecture. Please."

"Poor poppet, does your head still ache? I'll keep you only a moment, so you'll know what stories are being told. The servants' grapevine has a lot of headaches like yours but nothing worse among the ladies, who are swearing off sweets. The Almacks hostesses are investigating the punch bowls for signs of tampering. The shopkeepers consider the candies a national treasure, and the Lattimore sisters are a great success. Oh, and the Churchladies' Confectioners are out of business."

"We are? A success, I mean. I know we're out of business. I would never use that recipe again, you can be sure. I can close the books as soon as I collect on the last deliveries."

The viscount idly swung the tassels on his Hessians. "The books are closed. I packed up all the inventory, vats, molds, and supplies, and I bought all remaining stock at the stores. As I said, you are out of business."

Sydney was too drained to grow irate. Anger never seemed to get her anywhere with him anyway. "But that was my business. You had no right."

"No? I seem to recall a certain gift that I wished to give you. You kept insisting it was a loan, remember? In effect I bought the Churchladies' business from you in exchange for the debt. Now we are even."

Sydney's brows were furrowed as she thought about that. Either her brain was still drugged or his reasoning was as suspect as his character. "That doesn't make sense. I started the business with your money. Then you ended the business and saved my neck, with your money. The way I see it, I not only owe you my gratitude, I owe you twice as much money!"

"Dash it, Sydney, you can't still believe I make my living by collecting a pound of flesh!"

"Well, no," she conceded, "but you were there, and you did give me the gold."

"And I should have told you right away. All right. My brother was cheated and I went to retrieve his vouchers from the dastards. The thousand pounds I gave you was the payment for his misbegotten debt."

Sydney jumped up. "Then I owe the real money-lenders the money?" she squeaked. "And they are charging me interest while you sit here and blather on about punch bowls and patronesses?"

He stood too, and brushed a wayward curl off her forehead. "I don't blather, Mischief, and no, you don't have to worry about the Ottos. They are out of business, also. Out of the country, if they know what's good for them. So will you forget about the money once and for all?"

Sydney wished she could. Oh, how she would like to be unbeholden, especially to this man who kept her in such a flutter. But, "I cannot," she said. "I borrowed it in good faith, and swore to repay it on my honor. If I do not, then I shall have no honor. But don't worry," she told him in a brighter tone, "the Season is not yet over."

"And you have a plan. Now, where have I heard that before? But, sweetheart, a few more such schemes and you will owe me your soul." She was still looking soft and dreamy, so he couldn't help adding, "Just how much is your virtue worth?"

Her mouth opened to give him the setdown he deserved—so he kissed her.

Sydney was lost, and never more at home. Her toes curled in her slippers, and her hands reached up to touch his face, to feel his skin. Every church bell that ever rang in every steeple was chiming in her heart—or were those fire alarms clanging in her fuddled mind? What was she doing, enjoying herself in this shameful manner? Winifred still needed to make a good marriage, and Lord Scoville would be horrified. Heavens, Sydney thought, *she* would be horrified! She bit down hard where the tip of his tongue happened to be playing on her lips. He jumped back, cursing, and waited for the slap.

It never came. Sydney felt as much to fault because she hadn't pushed him away before, though she sensed he would have released her at the first hint of reluctance. She had stayed, sharing the kiss and thrilling to his nearness. She was disappointed in herself, and in him.

"You may not be a moneylender, but you are not a gentleman. I was right, wasn't I? You're still a rake."

The viscount was trying to rid his mouth of the taste of blood and his blood of the taste of her mouth. That's how well he was thinking. "I am not a rake," he declared firmly, then surprised himself by amending, "except where you are concerned."

"Why?"

"Why except for you? Because I am not interested in marriage but, God help me, I am interested in you. And why you? The devil only knows. You're the most wayward, troublesome female I've ever known. You're too young, too impetuous, too independent. And I can't seem to keep my hands off you."

That could almost be a compliment. Sydney grinned. "I think you are nice too, sometimes."

He lightly kissed the top of her nose and then smiled. "Didn't I tell you everyone likes me? At any rate, I have business in Sussex, so I'll be out of your hair for a while. Before I go, though, I want you to make me a promise." He was beginning to recognize her stubborn look, so he addressed her as he would a seaman contemplating mutiny: "By your own say-so, miss, you are in my debt. Therefore *I* name the terms, *I* call the play. You will promise to stay out of trouble, period. Nothing illegal, dangerous, or scandalous. Is that understood?"

Sydney was tempted to salute and say "Aye, aye," but she did not think he would be amused. She also did not think he would understand that she mightn't be able to keep such an oath. She compromised with the truth: "My next idea is none of those."

He was two blocks away before he realized she hadn't promised at all.

Aunt Harriet bustled over the next morning, top o'er trees at her nieces' success. "Lord Mayne, my dears. Just think!" Sydney did, and thought how shallow the *beau monde* was, that it could admire such a man. If they only knew what a libertine he was! Then again, if they only knew what a wanton *she* was, for welcoming the liberties he took, she'd be back in Little Dedham before the cat could lick its ear.

Lady Windham, however, deemed his lordship worth her paying the Lattimores' admission to Vauxhall, in case he was there. Naturally Sydney did not inform her aunt that the viscount was in the country; she wanted to see the fireworks. Unhappily Lord Mainwaring had stayed in town and

Lady Windham invited him to make up one of the company in their box.

"I wish you would not encourage him to dangle after Winifred, Aunt Harriet," she said. "I do not believe he is at all the thing. He may even run away to join the army or something."

"Nonsense, his mother would never allow it. If he does put on a uniform, I'm sure she'll see it's a general's." Furthermore, Lord Scoville's nose was out of joint at being cut out in Winnie's affections by a green boy. He was paying *his* attention to Beatrix, so Lady Windham was not about to dampen Lord Mainwaring's ardor. "Whatever can you be thinking of, Sydney? We wouldn't want to do anything to offend Lord Mayne."

Sydney almost choked on her arrack punch. Everything she did seemed to offend the man!

Lady Windham was carried away with dreams of finally getting Trixie off her hands. If she threw the young people together often enough, Scoville would see his case with Winifred was hopeless. He was bound to settle on Beatrix with her better breeding and larger dowry. It was just a matter of planning some small entertainments, picnics and such, where he wouldn't be distracted by yet another pretty face. Nothing too extravagant, mind. And of course Sydney could help send out the invitations and plan the menus.

"What was that, Aunt Harriet? I'm sorry, I must have been wool-gathering. No, I'm afraid I won't be able to help with your plans for an excursion to Richmond, although I would love to go if I have the time. You see, I am going to be busy with a project of my own which already has Lord Mayne's approval. We wouldn't want to offend him, would we?"

16

The Pen and the Sword

Grandfather was a famous general. Everyone
wanted to hear his adventures. Sydney happened
to have reams and reams of closely written pages
the general had penned right after his retirement
and before his last seizure. She put the two together and came up with the answer to her difficulties. She'd sell the general's memoirs and they
would all become rich.

Sydney had not read past the first pages, which
concerned themselves with the background history
of the Mahratta Wars, geographical details and cat-
alogs of the various artillery and troops. She recalled bedtime stories from her childhood, however,
tales of elephant hunts and native uprisings, towns
under seige and man-eating tigers. She had been
spellbound at the time—it was a miracle she did not
have nightmares to this day—and was positive others would be equally as fascinated with the general's heroic account. Even his descriptions of the odd
customs and religious practices were sure to cap-

ture the imaginations of any who read them, especially if they were like Sydney, who itched to see foreign lands. *Narratives of a Military Man* simply could not fail; it was only a matter of finding the publisher who would pay the most.

Sydney was very methodical about her quest. The general would have been proud at how she first scouted the terrain. She visited the lending library and studied all the titles in the history section. She copied down the names of a few publishers who seemed to specialize in past wars. Then she surveyed the biographical works, noting which companies produced volumes with the most elaborate embossing on the covers or the most gold leaf. She reasoned that these denoted a solvent operation. Furthermore, she firmly believed that an attractive cover had a great deal to do with a book's sales. Combining the two lists produced Sydney's primary targets.

Then she armed herself. She was not parading off to battle dressed like a pastel ingenue at Drury Lane. She and Annemarie designed a fashionable walking gown of forest-green cambric, with tight-fitting spenser to match. Not unintentionally, the short jacket had military-style buttons and epaulets on the shoulders. She wore a small green bonnet with gold braid trim and a wisp of net veiling which, Winifred assured her, added at least two years of maturity.

The campaign began. Sydney marched to the office of Watkins and Waters, Publishers. Her escort convoy, Wally, was two steps behind, proudly bearing the precious manuscript like a standard.

Sydney introduced herself to the clerk and told him she wished to inquire about the publication of a book. When he stopped ogling her, the flunky replied that if she made sure her name and direction were on the package, he would see that someone looked at it and returned the manuscript to her with a decision, in a month or two.

"I am sorry, sir, but you do not understand. I need a decision"—she needed a check—"long before then."

The clerk laughed and pointed to the area behind him. Manuscripts, some bound with string, some in leather portfolios like hers, some in cloth satchels, were stacked from the floor to above her height, several rows deep, across the width of the room.

The general's granddaughter was not to be defeated at the first skirmish. She withdrew one of her calling cards and insisted the clerk bring it to the instant attention of Mr. Watkins.

"Dead."

"Then Mr. Waters."

"Dead."

"Then whoever *is* in charge."

"That'd be Mr. Wynn, but he doesn't see anybody."

"He'll see me. You tell him that I am General Harlan Lattimore's granddaughter and ... and a friend of Viscount Mayne's."

Whether due to her glowing account of the general's adventures or her inspired use of the viscount's name, Mr. Wynn agreed to look at the memoirs himself.

"But we do not have a great deal of time," she prompted him. Mr. Wynn took that to mean the general was soon to join Mr. Watkins and Mr. Waters, and he vowed to read the pages that very evening.

Sydney was able to enjoy her afternoon's outing to the British Museum with Lord Thorpe even more, with victory in sight.

True to his word, Mr. Wynn had the package delivered to Park Lane the very next day. Unfortunately, he also sent his regrets that he was not able to offer to publish such an unfinished work. Since he understood time to be a critical factor, he could only wish her luck with the worthwhile venture.

"How dare the man call your writing unfinished!" Sydney fumed, sharing the note with her grandfather. He pounded his chair. "What did he expect from a military man anyway, Byron's deathless prose? Well, I am sure there are other publishers with a better sense of what readers want. If they wanted poetry, they would not be buying a war memoir in the first place."

Once more into the fray marched the troops. Hardened by her first battle, Sydney did not waste time with the clerk; she invoked Grandfather's rank and Lord Mayne's title. She was ushered into the senior partner's office at once and promised a quick reading.

Within days the hefty tome was returned, this time with a polite disclaimer: although the first chapter was as intriguing as Miss Lattimore had indicated, they would need to speak with the general in person before committing themselves to the project.

If the general could speak, he'd be out there trying to sell the blasted book himself. "Impertinent snobs!" Sydney raged. The general grunted and grred.

In no time at all Sydney hated all publishers,

hated the green dress, and hated those polite notes of rejection worst.

Only one publisher, the noted Mr. Murray, came in person. He asked for an interview with the general. Willy, minding the door that day, sent for Sydney.

Seeing tooled-leather volumes and pound notes dance in her head, Sydney hurried into the drawing room. "I'm so sorry," she temporized, "but my grandfather is resting. May I offer you tea?"

While she poured she nervously eyed the ominous package on the sofa beside the publisher. "What did you think of the memoirs?" she finally asked.

"I think they have great possibilities, Miss Lattimore, although they need a great deal more work, naturally. I understand the general is something of an invalid. Do you think he is up to so much more writing?"

Sydney knew for a fact he wasn't. He could barely hold a pen, much less dictate. She gnashed her teeth and promised to discuss Mr. Murray's suggestions with the general. She thanked the publisher for his time—and kicked the door after he left.

As she told her friend the next morning, those publishers and editors were all just disappointed writers who thought they could do better.

Mrs. Bella Ott nodded her head sagely and agreed.

Sydney had not seen as much of Mrs. Ott as during the candy-making days. She was out most times when Bella called, on her rounds of publishers or enjoying her new popularity. In addition, she could not feel easy with the woman after the mingle-mangle with the chocolate. Bella was the experienced cook; she should have noticed something was wrong with the recipe. No matter, she was a willing ear on this gray day of despond. A cold rain blew from the north, and there would be no gentlemen calling and no walks in the park. There were no more publishers for Sydney to try.

"Hogwash, dearie, you've just been going about it arsy-varsy. Did you offer them cash?"

"Money? Of course not. That's not the way it works. . . . Is it?"

"Girly, stop acting like you were born yesterday. That's the way everything works. New writers pay the publishers to get their books in print. You don't think book dealers are going to gamble their precious blunt on an unknown, do you? Not those cautious chaps. Didn't that poet fellow Byron have to scrape up enough to publish the first scribbles himself before his name became an instant seller? That's how it goes. Subsidies, it's called. A writer or his family or a friend of his, a patron-like, puts up the ready. I bet that Mr. Murray was sitting here sipping your tea, waiting for you to flash a golden boy or two. Instead, you give him another sticky bun."

"I never thought. Uh, how much money do you think it would cost?"

Bella hefted the packaged memoirs. "Big book like that, I reckon thousands."

"Thousands! But then how could we make any money?"

"You really are a green 'un. It's the publishers who make the money. Good thing Mrs. Alquith wrote me about you."

"Mrs. Asquith," Sydney corrected her absently, pondering this new dimension to her own ignorance. "We could never afford even one thousand, not after the loss on the confectionery business."

Bella did not want to talk about the candy venture. Hell, no one wanted to, it seemed. She and her boys had tried their best to get the rumor mills grinding. Granted the boys' best wasn't any great shakes, but no one would listen. Viscount Mayne had his story battened down so right and tight, no whispers were going to shake it. One of the scandal sheets even had the nerve to ask for proof that a parcel of chits had tried to drug the ton. Proof? Since when had truth ever had tuppence to do with what they published? Since one of the most powerful noblemen in the land got involved, they told her, that's when. Slander was one thing, they said, suicide was another.

There were other roads out of London, as the saying went. Things weren't hopeless yet, not by a long margin. She patted Sydney's hand. "Things ain't hopeless yet, my dear. Bella's here."

Bella knew a man. Among her wide acquaintance was the nephew of Lady Peaswell. ("No, she don't attend Almacks; she raises cats in Yarmouth.") Bella looked after this young man the same as she looked after Mrs. Asquith's young friends. She even cooked for him sometimes. It just so happened that this enterprising young man, of good family but needing to support himself, was just starting a printing and publishing business. All of his capital had gone for the equipment and rental for his new shop, so he was looking for material to publish—by subscription. He just might be willing to share the expenses with Sydney, and the profits, of course. It would only cost her, oh, maybe five hundred pounds, Bella thought, especially for friends. But Sydney would still see vastly more income if the book sold well than the pittance an established publisher would pay. Sydney needed a publisher and Bella's young friend needed a best seller to get him started. So what did dear Miss Sydney think? Sydney thought she couldn't wait to meet this enterprising, innovative young entrepreneur.

"Fine, fine. Why don't we go visit his office? You can get a look-see at the place and show him the pages. That way he can get the presses rolling, haha."

"Right now, in the rain?" Sydney wouldn't get in Bella's carriage with that impossible coachman on a clear day. She surely would not trust his driving on slippery roads with bad visibility. "I, ah, felt a tickle in my throat and thought I should stay inside today, the weather being so foul and all."

"Right you are, dearie. 'Sides, if I take the book to him on my way home, you'll have a decision that much sooner. And if Mr. Murray can call in person, so can Mr. Chesterton."

Mr. Oliver Chesterton was not quite what Sydney had expected in her daring new partner. Then again, he certainly was dressed creatively.

Chester refused to wear his own clothes when Bella insisted he had to look ink-stained, and the only chap his size to die that week was a Macaroni who'd succumbed to wet pavement and high heels. They managed to get the wheel marks off the checkered Cossack trousers. So there Chester was for his appointment with Miss Lattimore and her five hundred pounds, in black and white trousers, a puce coat, and cherry-striped waist. He had a huge boutonniere and shirt collars starched so high he could barely turn his head. His thin hair was slicked back with pomatum, and a rat-brown mustache was affixed under his nose. The false hair tickled, so he'd kept trimming it until the thing looked more like a rattail on his lip. He wore thick spectacles to make him look more bookish. Like Bella said, now he could stop looking for Lord Mayne behind every bush; he couldn't see the bush.

Before he left, Randy had spattered him with ink and then dipped each of his fingers in the pot. Everyone knew printers had ink under their fingernails, he said. Bella said he looked more like an acrobat she saw at a fair once, who walked on his hands right through the cow-judging tent.

If it weren't for the glasses, the ink, and Mrs. Ott's recommendation, Sydney would have thought him a park saunterer at best, a cardsharp at worst. She supposed his nasal accent was from Yarmouth, and his reed-thin frame a result of investing his life's savings in his business. He was assuredly not a reference for Bella's cooking.

Bella made the introductions and Mr. Chesterton reached out to shake her hand, curiously with his left. When that awkward moment was past and Mr. Chesterton found his seat, he got down to business. For a thousand pounds he would publish the book and she would keep all profits. For five hundred, they would split the earnings.

"I do think the manuscript has great possibilities, Miss Lattimore, so I would be willing to gamble," Mr. Chesterton offered. Mrs. Ott snorted into her tea. "But I do need the money in advance, you realize. I need to buy tickets—I mean, type faces."

This was a big decision. For once in her life Sydney wasn't eager to leap headfirst into unknown waters. Perhaps the fact of Chesterton leaving ink stains like pawprints on her mama's good china had something to do with it. Perhaps Lord Mayne's lectures had finally paid off. Then again, perhaps she only needed more time to decide between the five-hundred or thousand-pound arrangement.

Sydney told her guests that since it was such a major investment, she would have to consult the general and, no, she did not feel the need to inspect the premises.

"Thank you for coming in person, Mr. Chesterton," she told him, holding out her hand. She held out her left hand, assuming there must be something amiss with his right.

Chester never saw her hand at all. "I won't need to call again, will I? I mean, you can just send a check. Unless you change your mind about visiting us. Ma—Madam Ott can bring you."

17

Trust and Treachery

The general did not like any of the choices. Either that or he had something stuck in his throat. Wally, on duty that day, did not like the cut of Chesterton's jib. And Winifred did not understand the dilemma at all.

"But, Sydney, if we do not have enough money for the rest of the Season, why don't we just go home?"

"Because we would never have the chance to leave home again. Because Grandfather's pension will not be ours forever, and because you have the opportunity to make a good alliance."

"But what if I do not want to make a fine marriage, Syd? What if I thought being an officer's wife would suit me better, or a gentleman farmer's?"

A pox on both the Mainwaring brothers, Sydney thought, ripping up another note to the viscount. Drat the smooth-talking rake who could turn a girl's head, and drat his younger brother too.

She tried another sheet of stationery. She couldn't even decide on the salutation! *Dear Lord Mayne*, or *My dear Lord Mayne*? Stuff! Where was the cursed man when she needed him? Brennan said he was back in town. Wasn't it just typical of the contrary cad to make her write to ask his advice, when *he* was the one always mouthing propriety at her? Even Sydney knew it was totally improper for a young lady to be writing to a gentleman's residence. And heavens, she did not want to write this letter!

It was humiliating enough that she needed his money, and worse that she needed his name for entry to the publishers. Now she needed his advice as a man about town, and swallowing all the pages she had shredded would be easier than swallowing her pride. It wasn't that she wanted to see him, she told herself, just that she needed to see him. And he hadn't called.

She started again: *Your Lordship*.

Forrest Mainwaring despised gossip. He hated it worse when his name was mentioned. He was not in town over two hours when the gossip caught up to him. Something about his protégé, Miss Lattimore, of course, but how much of a hubble-bubble could even Sydney get into with the general's memoirs? He needed another day to track his friend Murray through the coffee shops before he had his answer. A partial answer anyway.

The next morning he went for a hard ride on a half-broken stallion. Later he worked out at Gentleman Jackson's. After luncheon at White's he took on Brennan in a fencing match at Deauville's. Now, he felt, he was ready to face Miss Sydney Lattimore. He was too physically and mentally drained to lose either his temper or his self-control.

He hadn't counted on the joy written on her face when she flew down the stairs to greet him, wearing a Pomona green muslin gown that swirled close to her rounded limbs. His traitorous body overcame exhaustion and rose to the occasion.

"You came!" She beamed, for she never had gotten around to posting a note. "You must have known I needed your advice."

Her smile made him feel like a slug for putting the visit off so long. Hell, he would have put it off for a lifetime rather than tie himself in knots like this. Nevertheless, he flicked a speck of lint off his sleeve and drawled at his most blasé, "Never tell me the indomitable Miss Lattimore has at last recognized the need to consult wiser heads about something."

She giggled at his affected manner, and his resolve to keep his distance fled. Ignoring her chaperone, the general fast asleep in his Bath chair across the room, Forrest sat on the sofa next to her instead of the chair opposite. He draped his arm across the back, where he just might touch the nape of her perfect, graceful neck. What was lower than a slug? He sighed, got up, and moved his seat. Polishing his quizzing glass, he wondered, "This mightn't have anything to do with a certain manuscript, would it?"

"Yes. You see, I've had this wonderful offer, but it is not quite wonderful, I think, and I thought—" But she never wrote the note, asking him to call. Uncertain, she asked, "That is, how did you know? I suppose my pea-wit of a sister mentioned it to Lord Mainwaring."

"She may have, but that's not how. I merely had to visit my club to hear your name—and mine—on everyone's lips."

Sydney felt the need to inspect her kid half-boots. "I, ah, didn't think you'd care. That is, no one would speak to me otherwise, and you said how much influence you have, and it was not dangerous, illegal, or scandalous, so I cannot see why you mind."

"It's not so much that I mind, poppet, as I do not understand what you were trying to do. No one does."

The "no one" was ominous. Sydney rushed on. "What is so difficult? I was trying to get the general's memoirs published, and received nothing but insults at first, your name or not. If certain persons were so quick to inform you I was trading on our acquaintance, for which I do apologize since you don't seem best pleased—but then, you never are, are you?—they should also have mentioned the poor treatment I received. Why, if they wanted money, those publishing gentlemen should have been above board about it like Mr. Chesterton, instead of maligning the general's work."

As usual when dealing with Miss Sydney Lattimore, the viscount felt he was missing something crucial. Perhaps he'd been watching her lips too carefully and hadn't heard an important fact. Then again, he'd always believed she was the one missing something important, in her brain box.

"Hold, Mischief. I spoke to Murray and he had only high praise for the general's writing."

"You know Mr. Murray?"

"Yes, he's a good friend. He was eager to ask me about the manuscript, knowing I had an interest in this quarter. He was most desirous of talking to the

162

general or finding out if there were any notes, or anyone else who might be able to finish the work."

"F-finish it?" The color had left Sydney's face, leaving a row of freckles across her nose.

"Do you mean you never read it, you goosecap? You were trying to peddle a book you never read?"

"I—I read the first few pages. There wasn't time, and I knew all the adventures anyway. The first chapter was full of dry-as-dust details."

"Then you would not have liked the rest of the book any better, Mischief, for they were all the same chapter! According to Murray, some gave more attention to the battles, some to other generals' viewpoints. But they were all the same chapter!"

Sydney did not understand. She was worrying her lip in that way she had of driving him to distraction. Forrest got up and turned his back on her to inspect a Dresden shepherdess on the mantel. "The general was a perfectionist, it seems, not a writer. He could never get the facts to come out like the exciting stories he used to tell his granddaughter, but he kept trying. Over and over. Murray says he would have done fine with a little guidance. It's too late now, isn't it?" he asked quietly.

Sydney just nodded.

"I'm sorry, Mischief," Forrest said, returning to her side, and she believed him.

She forced a tremulous smile. "It was a good plan, though, wasn't it?"

He raised her hand to his lips. "One of your best, sweetheart."

Sydney felt a glow spread through her—and then a raging inferno. She snatched her hand away and

163

jumped to her feet. "Why, that miserable, contemptible, low-down—"

"Murray? I swear he didn't—"

"No, Mr. Chesterton, the publisher! He liked the book! He said it was sure to be a best seller. He was going to print it with brown calf bindings and little gold corners—with my money! Why, that mawworm was trying to diddle me out of my whole bank account! He must have heard how green I was from those other publishers, the bounder. Wait till I see him again. I'll—"

"Chesterton? You don't mean Otto Chester, do you? Pale, thin, nervous-looking chap?"

"He was pale and thin, but his name was definitely Oliver Chesterton. Why? Who is Otto Chester?"

Now the viscount was up and pacing. "An insect that I should have squashed when I had the chance! He's the associate in O. Randall and Associates. You remember, the backroom banker. Otto Chester is the double-dealer who cheated Bren, then handed his forged markers to Randall for collection. I never thought he'd have the guts or the gumption to—"

"To come after me for the money you stole from them!" Sydney screamed.

"I did not steal the bloody money," he shouted back. "I told you, they got it dishonestly, so they were not entitled to the blunt!"

"Well, I'll just inform them of that fact the next time they come to tea!"

The general jerked awake and looked around to see if they were under attack. Sydney tucked the blankets back around his knees and turned his chair so he could look out the window. She grabbed

Forrest's sleeve and dragged him to the other side of the room.

The viscount pried her fingers loose before his superfine was damaged beyond repair. "They are not coming anywhere near you. I'll see to that! And they'll be dashed sorry they ever tried, too."

Sydney clutched her hands together to keep from wringing them like a tragedy queen. "Couldn't I just give the money back? If I had it to give, I mean. What I haven't spent? Maybe they would go away then."

The viscount took on the expression a cat might wear once it has the mouse between its paws. "They'll be going away for a very long time."

Sydney laughed nervously. "Here I thought they were your partners. Can you imagine?"

"Don't start that again, Mischief. Fiend seize it, do I look like an Otto?"

Healthy, tanned, strong, and confident, he did not resemble Mr. Chesterton in the least. She shook her head and smiled up at him.

He brushed the back of his fingers across her cheek. "Thanks, sweetheart. Now, listen, I do not want you even to think about contacting this dirty dish or giving him a groat. I'll track him down and take care of everything. You don't have to worry. Trust me."

Trust me. Isn't that what the snake said to Eve? Besides, how could she trust a man who was branded a rake by his own lips? By his own lips on hers, if she needed more proof! She still was not sure he wouldn't hold her to personal repayment of the loan—very personal. She wasn't even sure she would refuse!

Of course she would, Sydney told herself firmly. On the other hand, it would be far better if she could dissolve the worrisome debt and never let the question come up. She wondered, alone in her room, what might happen if she were independent and able to meet Forrest more as a social equal. Not that Miss Lattimore from Little Dedham could ever be the equal of the lofty Lord Mayne, but a girl could dream, couldn't she? She'd once tamed some wild kittens. How much harder could it be to reform a rake?

It still came down to the money. Whether she owed a hardened libertine or hardened criminals, she was in one hard place. She was never going to be safe, one way or t'other, unless she paid them all back. But how?

Lord Mayne placed guards around Sydney's house, alerted the twins, and made sure his brother accompanied the young ladies whenever he could at night. Forrest had his men out searching for Randall, and he himself haunted low dives and gaming hells looking for Chester.

He was never going to find Chester, not unless he crawled under every bed in every row house in Chelsea.

"He can't be an outlaw," Bella gasped as Sydney waved the vinaigrette under her nose. "He's Lady Peaswell's nephew."

Sydney poured tea to calm the older woman's nerves after her attack of the vapors. "I'm sorry, Mrs. Ott, but for all your town bronze, you were taken in the same as I was. The man is a charlatan, a professional gambler, and a cheat."

"Poor, poor Lady Peaswell," Bella blubbered into her handkerchief.

"Yes, well, even noble families have their black sheep. You must not let titles and such affect your good judgment."

Bella thought of Lord Whitlaw, Chester's father, and blubbered some more. "How true, how true. And how foolish I have been, my dear, me with my simple, trusting nature. I fed the boy, took him to my hearth, introduced him to my friends! Oh, how could I have been so blind? And how can I ever make it up to you, dear Sydney? Tell Bella what I can do so you'll forgive me for bringing a viper to your nest."

"Well, I have this plan. . . ."

18

Hell and Beyond

A polite hell was not one in which the sinners helped lace each other's ice skates. *That* was a cold day in hell, which was about when Miss Sydney Lattimore should have attended Lady Ambercroft's salon.

Lady Ambercroft was a young widow making a splash in the ton and a small fortune for herself by turning her home into a genteel gaming establishment. A lady could play silver loo or dip into her pin money at the roulette table without rubbing elbows with the lower orders or sharing the table with her husband's mistress. (Unless that mistress was another woman of birth and breeding on Lady Ambercroft's select list of invitees.) There was, supposedly, no drinking to excess, rowdy behavior, or wagering beyond the house limits.

The elegant premises were visited by much of society—even Aunt Harriet considered going when she heard refreshments were free—and gossiped about by the rest.

Lady Ambercroft herself was a lively, attractive

woman who had married a foul-breathed old man for his money, then celebrated his demise by spending her hard-earned inheritance. She still had her looks, she still had the house, she was still celebrating. She was also still on all but the highest sticklers' guest lists, so Sydney had met her. Over braised duck at the Hopkins-Jones buffet two evenings before, Sydney asked Lady Ambercroft if she could attend one of her game nights. The widow had laughed gaily and said of course, whenever Miss Lattimore's Aunt Harriet brought her. Which was right back to when hell froze over.

Sydney chose to consider that an invitation, as long as she was well chaperoned. She chose to accept. Lady Ambercroft was making money, she was not ruined in polite society, and, best of all, she lived right around the corner from the Lattimores!

Sydney had no problem feigning illness to cry off Aunt Harriet's musical entertainment planned for that evening; listening to Trixie and her friends torture the pianoforte and harp always gave her the headache. She just claimed one in advance.

Sydney had a little trouble convincing Mrs. Ott. "If you want to play cards, dearie, we can just go to my digs. That'll be more the thing, don't you know. My coach is right outside."

It might be more *convenable*, but it would not serve Sydney's purpose at all. It would serve Bella's even less to see her thousand pounds slide into some other woman's purse. She tried again: "His lordship ain't going to like it."

"He won't know. We can slip out the back door and walk the half block. I intend to stay for only an hour."

Bella revised her plans. In an hour even a cabbagehead like this gel would have rough going to lose a thousand pounds, but she sure as sin could lose her reputation.

As soon as Winifred left with Lord Mainwaring and Wally, and Annemarie as duenna, Sydney hurried into her most sophisticated evening gown, an amber silk with a lower neckline than usual and little puffed sleeves. She put a black domino over that, and pulled the hood up to cover her easily identifiable hair.

Ten minutes later she realized her mistake. She recognized no one in the place, she was by far the youngest female, the play was intense, and Lady Ambercroft was not happy to see her. The merry widow was not best pleased to see an unfledged deb in her establishment. Word that she was gulling innocents could ruin her. The old quiz with Miss Lattimore looked more like a procuress than a chaperone, furthermore, and Lady Ambercroft was having none of that type of thing in her house. Except in her own bedroom, of course.

She gave Bella a dirty look and pulled Sydney's hood back up.

The rooms were fairly thin of company this early in the evening, so there were a lot of dark corners for Sydney to stand in to watch the play. Bella took a seat at the *vingt et un* table, whispering that Lady Ambercroft would get in more of a pucker if they didn't drop a little blunt her way. Sydney drifted from room to room, counting the number of tables, checking the spread at the refreshments area, noting how many servants waited on the players. Some of the men at the craps table began to notice her, elbowing each other and pointing to the "phantom lady." She moved on. At the roulette wheel she received suggestions that she stand behind this man or that to bring him luck. She shook her head and continued her survey, thankfully not understanding half of the comments that followed her.

In a short while Sydney felt she had all the information she needed. The only thing she was not sure of was whether the dealers were paid employees or guests. Foolishly, she asked the man standing next to her at the faro table. He threw his head back and brayed, reminding her of Old Jeb's donkey back home, yellow teeth and all.

"The little lady don't know the first thing about gaming, gents. What say we teach her?"

A weasel-faced man whose teeth were filed to sharp points grinned at her and got up so she could take his seat.

"No, no, I am only here to watch, gentlemen. My friend—"

"If your friend is that fat old beldam who was playing *vingt et un*, she took a fainting fit and got sent home in a hackney."

Sydney jerked around. "Poor Bella, I have to—"

"She's long gone. Message was, your footman would see you home."

"But I didn't bring a—"Sydney looked around at the leering faces. Oh, Lord, she was in the suds again"—a heavy purse."

"That's no problem, ghost lady," an obese, sweating man wheezed at her. "I'll stake you." He pushed a column of colored chips her way.

"No, I'm sorry, I cannot—" she tried to say, tried to go. But a dark-skinned man with a scar under his eye said she had to play one round, it was a house rule. Donkey-laugh stood behind her so she could not run, and a scrawny old woman in a powdered wig from the last century put a hand on her shoulder and pushed her into the chair. Sydney tried to smile. She only had to wait for Lady Ambercroft to come into the room after all, or for Bella to send one of the Minch brothers back for her. "Very well, gentlemen, my lady. One round it is."

Someone placed a drink in Sydney's hand. She sipped, then pushed the glass aside. Whatever that was, she did not need it now. She needed some warm milk in her own kitchen.

Play began. Sydney did not know the rules or the worth of her markers. She didn't know a shoe from a shovel, as far as cards went. Not to worry, her new associates were quick to reassure, they'd teach her fast enough. She tried to sort out the instructions, then decided it was wiser just to follow what the fat man did, since he had the highest columns of colored chips.

By the time the shoe or dealing box came her way, Sydney had a better idea what she was about, she thought. At least her stack of markers and coins had grown. Weasel kept leering at her, but Marie Antoinette was scowling. Her pile was dwindling, as was Scarface's. Sydney did not want to upset these people by taking their money, not when she was a rank amateur, so she stood to leave.

"Surely one round has passed, and I really must be going." She pushed the winnings in Fat Man's direction. "Your stake, my lord, and thank you. It's been an, ah, education."

"Not so fast, Lady Incognita, not when you have all our blunt." Scarface smiled at her, a horrid, twisted thing. She shuddered. Someone else, she could not tell who, said, "That's not sporting," and a third voice called, "That's the rules of the house."

The old lady laid a clawlike hand on Sydney's shoulder. Dear heaven, where was Willy? Sydney prayed. Where was Lady Ambercroft?

Lady Ambercroft was upstairs. Shortly after the unfortunate episode with Miss Lattimore's dragon, a small, long-toothed gentleman with red hair entered the premises. Lady Ambercroft did not know him, but his credentials gleamed in the candlelight: rings, fobs, a diamond stickpin. Lord Othric Randolph, wearing the late Lord Winchester Whitlaw's final bequest, looked around the rooms, nodded in satisfaction, then offered his hostess a private high-stakes game upstairs. One she couldn't lose.

Willy was at home in the butler's pantry, throwing dice with Lord Mayne's hired house-watcher. Lord Mayne was not happy about that either. Restless and edgy that no one had spotted Chester or Randall, the viscount had driven through a cold mist to Park Lane on his way to the clubs.

"Don't fatch yourself, milord," his paid guard told him, tossing the cubes from hand to hand. "I'm inside 'cause it came on to drizzle, and the little lady's safe as houses. Her and the sister went off with your brother"—a nod to Willy—"and your brother, milord, to her auntie's. Be back around midnight, I 'spect."

Willy shook his head. "No, that was Annemarie who went with Miss Winifred and Wally. Miss Sydney is upstairs with the headache."

Now the guard scratched his bald pate. "Iffen it was the maid who went with the others, who was it in the black cape what walked down the block with the old neighbor lady?"

A quick search had the viscount cursing and

stomping around the entry hall. Willy tried to convince him that Miss Sydney had a good head on her shoulders; she'd do fine.

"Fine? She hasn't done fine since I've known her! This time I am finished. Good riddance to bad baggage, I say. I told her, nothing dangerous, illegal, or scandalous. So what does she do? She skips off in the middle of the night going the devil knows where—for what? To rob the crown jewels, for all I know! To think I put a guard on the house to keep her safe! I should have chained the wench to the bed." He crammed his beaver hat down on his head. "Well, no more. She can come home looking like butter wouldn't melt in her mouth and those greenish eyes as innocent as a babe's. It won't work this time. I'm gone."

He turned back when the guard chuckled. "And you're fired. Pick up your check when you bring word that she's home safe."

His club was nearly empty. Some older types were playing whist, and a group of dandies were tasting each other's snuff mixtures in the bow window.

"Where is everybody?" Forrest asked a solitary gentleman sprawled in one of the leather chairs with a bottle by his side.

"Those who couldn't avoid it are at Lady Windham's musicale. Bunch of others are at the new production at Covent Garden. New chorus girls." He poured himself another drink. "And those whose dibs are in tune," he said with a grimace for the sneezes from across the room and the state of his own finances, "are at that new hell of Lady Ambercroft's that's all the rage."

Now that was more the thing, the viscount decided, smiling fondly at memory of a romantic interlude with Rosalyn Ambercroft. Lady Ros was just what he needed to rid his mind of Sydney Lattimore once and for all, even if it meant going out into the damp night again.

Lady Ambercroft was unavailable, the butler informed him when he took the viscount's hat, gloves, and cane. Perhaps if Lord Mayne visited the card rooms, her ladyship might be free later, the servant suggested with a wink.

And perhaps pigs would fly before Viscount Mayne stood in line for a doxie's favor, no matter how highborn. Ah, well, he was already here. Forrest thought he may as well have a drink or two of Rosalyn's finest cognac just to take the chill off, and see if there was any interesting play going on.

He put a coin down on red, even, at the wheel, then strolled away, not waiting to see if he won. He played a hand or two of *vingt et un*, decided he did not like the dealer's lace cuffs, and moved on.

There seemed to be a stir around the faro table, so the viscount headed in that direction, stopping at the dice game to bet on his friend Collingwood's nicking the main. Forrest jingled his winnings in one hand as he made his way to the faro table.

All seats were taken and spectators were two deep behind the players. The viscount moved around the side, where his height would let him view the action. He idly reached for another drink from a waiter's tray, then turned back.

Coins rolled unnoticed to the thick carpet. The glass slipped through Lord Mayne's fingers, spilling wine on his white Persian satin breeches. "Oh, hell."

19

Reputation Roulette

It was dark, her hood was up. He couldn't be sure. Then she turned and one of those blasted Pekingese-colored curls glimmered in the candlelight.

The viscount was going to walk away. This time he really was. If Miss Lattimore wanted to play ducks and drakes with her good name, that was her business, none of his.

"Please, gentlemen," he heard her say as he walked past, a quaver in her voice, "I really do not want to play anymore. See? I have no money left. You've won it all back, so you cannot say I was a poor sport." The viscount's feet refused to take another step, no matter what his head ordered.

A sharp-featured man said they'd take her vowels, and that fat old court-card Bishop Nugee claimed she owed him twenty pounds, for his stake. Lord Mayne was prepared to let Sydney stew a while, to teach her a lesson. Then he saw someone put his hand on her shoulder. Then he saw red.

The viscount brushed the spectators aside like flies.

"No, I did not owe anyone," Sydney declared. "I won't take any of your money or your advice. I am going home." She did not know if these scoundrels would let her; she did not know if her legs would carry her. She did not even want to think about walking out of there on her own, in the dark, with no one beside her. Grandfather always said never show fear, so she raised her chin. "I do not think you play fair." Just then someone tossed a roll of coins over Sydney's shoulder toward the bishop. She turned to refuse before she was in deeper water, if that was possible. Or if it mattered, now that she was drowning anyway. "I didn't . . ." The words faded when she saw who stood behind her chair.

The breath she did not know she was holding for the last hour or so whooshed out of her. Safe! Like dry land to a shipwrecked sailor, like a sip of water to a sun-drenched jungle wanderer, rescue was at hand. Sydney almost jumped up and hugged her savior, until she got a better look at Lord Mayne's granite face and saw the whitened knuckles clenched around the rungs of her chair back. Like a shark to the shipwrecked sailor, like a tribe of cannibals to the soul lost in the jungle, some fates were worse than death.

Sydney fumbled in her reticule for the few shillings she carried there. "On second thought, I think I shall play a bit more."

Another roll of coins landed on the table, this time right in front of her. "New cards," she heard him call like the sound of doom. "The lady deals."

* * *

Sydney did not have to concentrate on the rules or the cards or her bets. The viscount tapped his quizzing glass on the card he wanted her to play, and just as silently indicated how much she should wager. No one else spoke, for the gamblers had to look to their own hands rather than count on a rigged game to pluck the little pigeon of every feather she had. Now the dark lady held the deal and Mayne's reputation kept them honest. No one dared to mark the cards or switch them. It was a fair game.

There were no more ribald comments and no taunts aimed at flustering Sydney, which would have been too late by half anyway. Her hands made the motions of passing cards from the shoe to the players, pushing forward the coins and markers, collecting the winnings. As the pile in front of her grew, so did her trepidation at the unnatural silence. She thought they must all hear her knees tapping together or the frantic pounding of her heart or the drops of nervous perspiration slipping down her back. She had to wipe her hands on her cloak to keep the cards from sticking to them.

"Please." She turned to beg when it seemed the game would go on for another lifetime. "Please may I go home now?"

The viscount gestured to a hovering servant who immediately produced a silk purse, into which he scraped the winnings. The rattle of the coins was the only sound. The viscount pushed some of the markers aside for the house share and some for the servants, then nodded for one of the dealers to exchange the rest for cash. Only then did he pull back Sydney's chair and help her to rise with a hand under her elbow. He kept it there as he guided her out of the hushed room. She could hear the whispers start behind them, but Lord Mayne kept walking at a measured pace, not hurrying. And not talking. He nodded to some of his friends, cut others who tried to catch his attention. Sydney hadn't realized the rooms were five miles long!

Finally they reached the entryway, which was empty except for the butler and some footmen. Forrest merely had to dip his head for his cane, hat, and gloves to be handed over, his carriage sent for, the winnings carried to him.

That sack of coins seemed to loose the flood of words he'd been striving to contain until they were alone. Shoving it into Sydney's hands, too furious to care who heard, he growled: "Here, madam. I hope the gold was worth this night's cost. You have gambled away your reputation, gambled away your sister's future, all to repay a debt no one wanted."

"But, my honor—"

"Your honor be damned. There was no dishonor in accepting a gift when you needed it, only a blow to your stubborn pride. And what is honor but your good name? You have done everything in your power to see yours dragged through the mud, blast you."

Sydney was trembling, his arm the only thing keeping her standing. Still, she had to make him understand. "But the household was counting on me! What else could I do when they all depend on me?"

"You can bloody well let me take care of you!" he shouted for the edification of the servants, the gamblers who were crowded in the doorway to watch, the butler who stood holding the door, and the three carriages passing by.

Scarlet-faced, Sydney shook off his arm. "Thank

you, my lord. Now we can *all* be assured my ruination is complete." She loosened the strings of the purse and tipped it over, coins spilling at his feet and rolling across the marble foyer, pound notes fluttering in the breeze from the still-open door. One footman maintained his pretense of invisibility; the other scurried crabwise along the floor to collect the bills and change.

"And as for the winnings, my lord, I do not want anything from either you or this foul place. I did not earn it, I shall not earn it, and I would not take it—or you—if I were starving. If my sister was forced to take in washing," she shouted as she ran through the open door, past the open-mouthed butler. "If Grandfather had to reenlist. If Wally had to wrestle bears. If Willy had to . . ." Her voice faded as she was swallowed up in the dark, rainy night.

"That's not what I meant," the viscount murmured, but only the footman handing him the refilled purse heard. Lord Mayne absently handed him a coin, then he looked at the crowd gathered in the hallway and repeated so they could all hear: "That's not what I meant." The bishop nodded and held his finger alongside his nose. The rest of them leered and winked. "Blast. Very well, let me put it this way: Nothing untoward occurred tonight. Anyone who believes differently had better be prepared to meet me. Likewise anyone who might feel the need to mention the lady's name, if you know it, had best be ready to feel cold steel. Swords, pistols, fists, it matters not. And now good night, gentlemen."

Forrest called her name and Sydney walked faster. He caught up with her before she reached the corner of Park Lane and did not stop to argue. He scooped her up and tossed her and the silk purse into his carriage. Before getting in, he ordered the driver to go once around the park before returning Miss Lattimore to her home. Then he took the seat across from her, his arms crossed on his chest.

Sydney pulled her cloak about her. She was damp, chilled, and shaken, now that her anger was not heating her blood. For sure she was not going to receive any warmth or comfort from Lord Mayne, sitting there like a marble sculpture, handsome and cold. The streetlights showed the muscle in his jaw pulsing from being clenched so tightly.

"I won't take it," Sydney said quietly, moving the purse to his side. "It would make me feel soiled." He nodded. She continued: "And I shall repay the loan, for I do not wish to be beholden to you."

He nodded again. "So I surmised. But tell me, did you really intend to finance the rest of your sister's Season, support your household, and reimburse me, by gambling? Not even you could be so addled to think that. Don't you know the house always wins? You would only end up more in debt, losing what you had to start."

Sydney gathered some dignity around her—it was more rumpled than her sodden cloak—and pulled a small notebook from her pocket. "I have never been the wantwit you consider me, my lord. I did not go there to gamble, but to observe. I wanted to know how such an enterprise was run. See? I made note of the staff and the rooms and tables. I thought that if things got desperate, we could turn the ground floor of our house into a gaming parlor, for invited guests only, of course."

The viscount's lip was twitching. "Of course."

"Don't patronize me, Lord Mayne. I was led to believe that only the highest ton were invited there. I admit I was wrong, but the principle is sound. As you said, the house always wins. I could see that Lady Ambercroft is making a fortune, and maybe I could too. She is providing for herself and she is still accepted everywhere."

Forrest was not about to discuss all the ways Lady Ros was earning her bread. "Lady Ambercroft is a widow, not a young deb. Furthermore, she is accepted, not necessarily welcomed, and that more for her husband's title and despite her present occupation. And finally, one of the places where she is not accepted and never will be is the marriage market. Gentlemen like Baron Scoville do not countenance their prospective brides shuffling pasteboards in smoky rooms. They don't even like to be related to in-laws in trade, Mischief, much less a sister who runs a gaming den."

"Oh, pooh, I scratched Baron Scoville off my list ages ago. I never liked him anyway, and Winnie seems determined on your brother. I thought we could use him as a dealer, since he is familiar with such places. That way we could save money on the staff and give him a respectable income so he doesn't have to make the army his career."

"A respectable—" He was laughing too hard to continue. "Mischief, your mind certainly works in mysterious ways. Bren has two small estates of his own and will come into a moderate fortune from our mother. The only reason he has not bought himself a commission, indeed why neither I nor my father has seen to it for him, is that Mother threatens to go into a decline if he signs up. She would purchase his cornetcy herself, however, rather than see him become a knight of the baize tables. But thank you, poppet, for worrying about my brother's reformation. As a croupier!"

While he was laughing again, Sydney thought about her plan to reform Forrest Mainwaring as well as Brennan. She could see her strategy needed more refining, especially since she could not resist laughing with him.

Lord Mayne moved over to her side of the carriage and put his arm around her. "Listen, Mischief, we are partners, more or less, aren't we?" Sydney allowed as how they might be. "Then I get to have a say in how the money is spent. That's fair, isn't it?" She nodded her head, dislodging the hood. He brushed the damp curls off her cheek. "Then I absolutely, categorically, forbid our blunt being used to set up a gambling den, no matter how polite. Is that understood?"

"You needn't worry, Lord Mayne, after tonight I would never consider such a thing."

"That's Forrest, sweetheart. I really think we are on familiar enough terms to stop my-lording and my-ladying each other."

Sydney felt they were on quite too familiar terms, her cheek tingling from his touch. She trembled and inched as far away from him as she could on the leather seat.

Forrest was not entirely convinced that she had abandoned her latest scheme. Reliving the horror of finding her in such a place, he said gruffly, "You know, having his granddaughter set herself up as a child of fortune would break the general's heart."

"Having a granddaughter instead of a grandson already broke his heart. I thought I'd let him op-

183

erate the roulette table," she said with a giggle. "No one could accuse him of stopping the wheel with his foot under the table."

Forrest did not think she was taking his warning seriously enough. "I swear, Mischief, if you ever mention starting such a place, if you so much as set foot in such a place, I'll turn you over my knee and beat some sense into you, which should have been done years ago. As a matter of fact, it's not too late." Seeing that she was shivering—from his threats or the cold—Forrest reached out to pull her onto his lap. Sydney screamed until he stopped her mouth with his.

Whatever sense she ever had flew right away, for she let him kiss her and hold her and touch her. And she kissed him and held him and touched him back, and enjoyed it mightily.

Such a heavenly embrace might have led heaven knew where, but they were home, and Willy—or Wally—was opening the door, looking mad as fire to find Missy sitting in his lordship's lap. The footman plucked her out like a kitten from a basket and stood glaring at the viscount. Forrest could not tell whether it was the twin with the glass jaw or not, and did not feel like finding out the hard way. He tapped his cane on the carriage roof and left, smiling.

The guard outside, his own paid watchman, called after the coach: "Lordy, you never said I was supposed to keep her safe from you!"

20

High Ton, High Toby

Sydney had a cold, and cold feet about meeting the ton. As soon as word spread that the younger Miss Lattimore was afflicted with a chill, however, even more bouquets of flowers arrived at Park Lane from suitors, along with baskets of fruit from well-wishers and pet restoratives from various dowagers. By some miracle—or Lord Mayne—Sydney had squeaked through another scrape with her reputation intact. She was too miserable to care.

Her nose was stuffed, her plans had gone awry, her heart was in turmoil, and her wits had gone begging. How could it be, she asked herself, that of all the men in London, she was attracted to one with no principles? How could it be that whenever she was with him she forgot her own? As for his taking care of her, he could do that when cows gave chocolate milk! Sydney blew her nose and pulled the covers over her head.

She refused to see any of the callers, except for one. Winifred came upstairs to beg her sister to grant Mrs. Ott an interview. "For you must know she is downstairs weeping and moaning about how it is all her fault that you are ill. I do not know how that could be since you were already feeling poorly before she came. Nevertheless, she refuses to leave until she sees with her own two eyes that you are recovering. Grandfather is becoming a trifle over-set at the commotion, Syd, and you know I hate it when he makes those noises."

Bella was indeed beating her breast, and the general was beating his fist on the arm of his chair when Sydney dressed and went down. She set Winnie to reading Grandfather the newspapers while she took Bella off to the front parlor for a glass of sherry and a cose.

"Oh, my dear, I am so ashamed! What you must think of poor Bella, going off and leaving you like that. But my nerves! You know I haven't been the same since the major passed on. It was that place what did it, the gambling, the men. Why, a man next to me lost twenty bob right there at one turn of the card, then said the game was as crooked as a goat's hind leg! My stars! My very heart took to palpitating. I knew we should leave. That was no place for ladies like us, I could see straight off."

"Yes," Sydney agreed, "we were sadly misinformed. I think there must not be such a thing as a polite hell. But why did you not come get me when you realized, especially if you were feeling ill?"

"I tried, dearie, Lord knows I tried. I was on my way to find you when a man pinched me! I won't call him a gentleman, I won't, but can you believe that?"

In the usual course of things, Sydney wouldn't. Bella was more pillowy than willowy. In her widow's weeds she looked like raw dough in a sack, puffy face dotted with raisin eyes. And for all her troubles, no one had taken such liberties with Sydney's person until the ride home, of course. Still, as she told Bella, refilling the other woman's glass, she was willing to believe anything was possible at Lady Ambercroft's.

Bella frowned, but went on. "Well, my heart started going *ga-thump, ga-thump, ga-thump*. I could hear it in my ears, I could! Then a black cloud passed right over my eyes. Like the time you told me that publisher chap was a sneakthief."

"Perhaps you should see a physician?"

"Oh, I have, dearie, I have." Or the next best thing, tipping a jug with the mortician next door. "He says emotional turmoil carries away a lot of folks. Anyways, next thing I know, Lady Ambercroft's man is calling for a hackney. But what about Miss Lattimore, I says? I can't just go leave the lamb. She says she'll look after you till I send your footman back to see you home. So I give the jarvey my address, and tell him to go by Park Lane so I can leave a message, and then—oh, I am too ashamed to tell!" She started striking herself on the chest again.

No wonder her heart went *ga-thump*, Sydney thought, if she kept pounding on it that way. "Please, Bella, please calm yourself. Remember what the doctor said. Just tell me what happened."

"A mouse."

"A mouse?"

"Recall how it was raining that night? The jarvey put down a fresh layer of straw to keep his coach clean from the wet boots and such. And I heard it, I swear."

"The mouse?"

"It's foolish, I know, but I am mortal afraid of mice, dearie. Why, my husband used to call me a chicken-hearted maid." (Paddy's actual words were "cheating-hearted jade," or worse.)

"I am sure he did not mean anything terrible by that...."

"But it's true, and I failed you, lovey, through being weak. I heard the mouse. Right at my feet, it was. And I couldn't help myself, I start screaming for the driver and jumping on the seat, and all the time my heart going *ga-thump, ga-thump*, and then that black curtain comes down again. Next thing I know, I'm in my own parlor, with m'footman burning feathers under my nose. Then I remembered! I never got that there message to your house! Well, I almost went off again, let me tell you. But before I did, before I even took a sip of spirits to settle my nerves, I sent my man round with a note. Tell me, dearie, tell Bella so I can stop worrying, he got there in time, didn't he, before anyone could insult you or"—her whole body quivered—"make improper advances."

"As you can see, I am perfectly fine," Sydney told her, somehow not comfortable repeating the evening's true events. "Willy got your message and was there in no time flat. Why, it seemed like just a few minutes after you left." Sydney was already on her way home with the viscount, though, and those were the longest few minutes of her life. There was no reason to disturb poor Mrs. Ott any more, however, so Sydney merely told her, "It was an unfortunate night, but we are neither much the worse for it, except for this wretched cold, so if you would excuse me ... ?"

"Of course, of course, dearie." Bella heaved herself out of the chair and ground her teeth. "We wouldn't want you to get an inflammation of the lungs or anything. But tell me, what of your plan to open a card parlor?"

"Oh, I can see that would be totally ineligible. In fact, I am surprised you didn't warn—No matter, I have decided to stop worrying about money and let tomorrow take care of itself."

Bella had never heard such tripe in her born days, no, not even from Chester. What else was a body supposed to worry about, if not having enough blunt for the future?

Happiness, that's what. Sydney realized she'd been putting her own pride in front of her sister's happiness, her own desire to avoid a loveless marriage ahead of Winnie's comfort. Facing the prosy Lord Scoville across the coffee cups for the rest of one's life would curdle anyone's cream. No, if Winnie wanted to marry Brennan Mainwaring, Sydney would not stand in their way.

When Brennan applied to the general for Winnie's hand, a conversation bound to be memorable, Sydney would have to be the one to take him aside and discuss settlements. If he truly had two estates, surely he could not object if Sydney and the general occupied one. In exchange, she would be the best aunt ever to his and Winnie's offspring, Sydney swore to herself. Nor should Mainwaring balk at repaying his own brother the funds that kept Winnie in muslins and lace, if he was as warm as the viscount claimed. Lord Mayne could return it as a wedding gift and they would all be satisfied.

Everyone but Sydney. The thought of spending

the rest of her life in the country tending to someone else's blue-eyed, black-haired babes, even Winnie's, was so depressing she took to her bed for another day.

After twenty-four hours of hot chocolate and purple prose from the lending library Sydney felt much better. Happily not well enough for Almacks, bless King George and the Minerva Press.

Forrest stayed away for two days. His absence may have defused some of the rumors connecting his name and Sydney's, but it did nothing for his peace of mind. He couldn't keep that mind off the impossible chit. The devil, he still couldn't keep his hands off her. He was besotted, he admitted it, a grievous state indeed. Lord Mayne tried to treat this affliction like any other illness or injury: wrap it up, drown it in spirits, and sleep it off, or else forget about it and get on with one's business. None of those remedies worked. He was neglecting his correspondence, relegating estate matters to the stewards, delaying financial decisions. And all for worrying over what bumblebath Mischief would fall into next.

Tarnation, the only way to keep the minx out of trouble was to keep her by his side. The idea of Sydney's tempests and tumults cutting up his well-ordered life on a daily basis was enough to make him shudder. Then he realized she was already doing it, driving him to distraction. Every day with Sydney? No, he shouted inside his own head, he did not want a wife! Especially not one who was impetuous, mercurial, and illogical, everything he held in low esteem. He had Brennan; he did not need a wife. He had a full and rich, satisfying existence; he did not need chaos in his life.

But every night with Sydney? *That*, perhaps, was exactly what he needed to cure this ailment.

It was Wednesday, it was Almacks. Why wasn't she here? Forrest surveyed the assembly hall through his quizzing glass, very well aware that he himself was the object of nearly every other eye. Blast, he thought, he'd done his best to see her vouchers to the boring place were not rescinded; the least she could do was not offend the patronesses by bowing out. Gads, if he could suffer being stared at and toadied to, fawned on and flirted with, discussed from his income to his unmentionables, then she could be there to waltz with him.

He waltzed with Sally Jersey instead. Her privileged position gave her the right to ask questions instead of speculating behind his back. Or so she believed.

"You would not be looking for anyone in particular, would you, darling?"

"Why would I, when I already have the loveliest lady here in my arms?"

"But twice in one month to the marriage mart? A lady might think you were on the lookout for a bride."

He twirled her in an elegant loop, ending the dance with a flourish. "My dear Silence, ladies should never think." He bowed and walked to where his brother was leading Winifred Lattimore off the floor.

"Miss Lattimore," he said, bowing over her hand with his usual easy grace. "You are as beautiful as ever. Parliament should send your portrait to the troops on the Peninsula to remind them what they are fighting for. I'll mention it to my father."

Instead of saying "oh, la," batting her eyelashes at him, or rapping him coyly with her fan, Winnie blushed and said, "Thank you, but I am sure those brave men need no reminding. Sydney says they would do better with sturdier boots, however, if you wish to pass that on."

Forrest could just imagine the duke's reaction to Sydney's well-founded suggestion that the war was not being efficiently managed. Not even the Ming vase would be safe. Then he considered how refreshing it was that neither of the Lattimore ladies flirted. He hoped the Season and the adulation would not change her—them.

"Miss Sydney keeps up with the war news, Forrest," Bren told him, "reading to the general. Well-informed, don't you know. She thinks I should reconsider wanting to join up. The war's liable to be over too soon for me to make a difference, she says."

If Forrest thought it curious that his heygomad brother listened to Sydney instead of his mother, father, and brother, he refrained from commenting. Instead, he remarked, "I must remember to thank Miss Lattimore, then. I, ah, do not see her among the gathering."

"No, she was too ill to join us," Winifred said. "She came down with an ague the night of Aunt Harriet's musicale. She should be recovered by tomorrow. Shall I tell her you asked for her?"

"Please." His heart sinking while he mouthed polite expressions of sympathy, Forrest turned to his brother. He remembered the last time Sydney cried off an engagement. She was too sick for Lady

Windham's, but well enough for Lady Amber-croft's.

Bren was reassuring. "You should have seen her, nose all red, eyes kind of glassy—ow." Winnie kicked him. "Uh, right. Lady and all, always in looks."

It was an odd infatuation when a gentleman was relieved to find the object of his affections ailing. Forrest smiled. A broken leg would have kept her out of trouble longer; a cold was good enough for now.

Forrest swung Miss Winifred into a *contre danse*, cheerfully cutting out Baron Scoville, whose name was on her card. Then he left, causing more of a buzz that he danced with only one young lady and grinned the whole time.

Lord Mayne went to White's, where he could relax in a male enclave, smoke a cheroot, sip a brandy, play a hand or two of piquet, all without a single worry to ruffle his feathers. He did keep his ears tuned to the flow of gossip, just in case Sydney's last hobble was mentioned. Nothing. He sighed with contentment and ordered his supper before the place got crowded.

When he returned from the dining room the club was in a frenzy with the latest tidings. Knowing Sydney was home safe in bed let the viscount stroll casually toward a knot of gentlemen who were shouting, waving their hands, and demanding action.

"The war?" he inquired of his friend Castleberry.

"No, highwaymen. Where have you been that you haven't heard? Last night five carriages were held up on Hounslow Heath. Three already tonight. It's all anyone can talk of."

"I don't see why. The authorities will have the gentlemen of the road under lock and key in jig time."

"But that's just it, Mayne. This new bunch is a gang of three: two men and a female!"

Talk swirled around the viscount, chatter about what was the proper term for the female robber: Highwaywoman? Footpadess? High Tabby? That dull dog Scoville arrived and surprised them all with a particularly vulgar expression to do with the bridle lay.

But Viscount Mayne was back in his chair, holding his head in his hands. He was closer to despair than any time since his navy days. He knew precisely what you called a female out on the roads at night, robbing carriages. You called her Sydney.

21

Low Road, Low Blow

*T*he viscount went home and put on his oldest coat and buckskin breeches. He took out his wallet and identifying cards lest he be held to ransom. Leaving only a few pounds in his pocket, he stuck two pistols in his waistband and called for his fastest horse. He rode out to Hounslow Heath through another dark, damp mist.

He was promptly arrested.

Two nights it took, and two days. Two nights in rat-infested, stinking cells with unwashed drunks and felons. Two days of loutish deputies, ignorant, sadistic sheriffs, pompous magistrates. Forty-eight hours he spent, with no sleep lest his boots and coat be stolen, and food he would not feed to swine. Then he was given the opportunity to make a total ass of himself before one of his father's political cronies, explaining why a notable peer of the realm was playing at highwayman.

He did not stop at his own home to rest, to eat,

to change his foul clothes, or to shave. He did not stop when Griffith tried to shut the front door in his savage face.

Bren jumped up from the parlor. "What happened to you, Forrest, and where the deuce have you been? I've been frantic."

Forrest looked toward the couch, where a blushing Winifred was attempting to repin her hair. "So I see," he said dryly.

Brennan bent to retrieve a missing hairpin. "It, ah, ain't what you think, Forrest. Chaperoned and all, don't you know." He jerked his head toward the general, half asleep in the corner.

Forrest knew the slowtop's goose was cooked. He did not care. "Where's Sydney?"

"She's out making calls. But don't worry," he added when he saw his brother's face go even more rigid, "she's got both of the twins with her."

Boiling in oil was too good for them. Being stretched on the rack was—

The general pounded on his chair. When he had Lord Mayne's attention he raised his trembling hand and pointed toward the rear of the house.

"Thank you, sir," Forrest said, bowing smartly. Only Mrs. Minch was in the kitchen, scouring a pot. She took one look at his lordship's stormy face and nodded toward the back door. Then she grabbed up the bottle of cooking wine and locked herself in the pantry.

In the rear courtyard, where a tiny walled garden used to be, was a gathering of liveried servants, footmen, and grooms. Forrest did not see them. Willy and Wally sat on one side of an old trestle table in their shirt-sleeves; he barely registered their presence. He had eyes only for Sydney, eyes

196

that narrowed to hardened slits when he got a good look at her.

Miss Lattimore was wearing her stable boy's outfit, wide smock, breeches, knitted hat. She was sitting on a barrel, smiling, laughing . . . and counting the stacks of coins and bills in front of her on an overturned crate.

The viscount roared and lunged for her, knocking aside the table, the crate, and the barrel. He yanked her up by the collar of her loose shirt and shook her like a rat.

Wally jumped to his feet, forming his huge hands into fists. Willy grabbed a loose tree branch.

"You stay back, both of you, and wait your turn," Forrest raged, still dangling Sydney in the air. "I'm looking forward to you for dessert. And don't worry, I'm not going to kill the little snirp. I'll leave that to the hangman."

They grinned and righted the table, leaving Sydney to her fate. She kicked out, trying to get free. "Put me down, you barbarian!" she screamed.

He did, only to clamp her shoulders in a viselike grip and shake her some more. "What . . . in bloody hell . . . do you think . . . you are doing?"

Sydney aimed her wooden-soled work boot at his shin, but missed. He squeezed harder. She would have marks for weeks, as if he cared. He hadn't even come to see her when she was ill. She tried to kick him again. "For your information, you brute, the boys and I have found a new source of income. We're taking on all comers at arm-wrestling. I am the bank."

His arms fell. "You're the . . ."

"The odds-maker and scorekeeper and timer. And I am quite good at it, too. And you can just stop breathing fire at me, my lord bully, because I never left these premises, and all of these men are friends. Besides, I had to find something to do when I looked too horrid to go to parties with my nose all red, and *no one* came to visit."

Her nose was indeed pinkish and puffy. She was indignant that he stayed away, an astounding enough discovery. "Did you really miss me?" he asked, and stepped back from another swipe of her boot.

"Then you weren't out on Hounslow Heath?"

"Of course not, there's a band of robbers out— why you, you dastard! You thought I was holding up carriages! You thought I would *steal* for money! You, you . . ." She couldn't think of words bad enough.

The viscount held up his hands. "Well, you kept thinking I was a loan merchant and a rake."

"You were, and you are!" she yelled, trying one last kick. This one connected quite nicely with his kneecap. She limped into the house while Willy tipped up the barrel and Wally helped the viscount to it.

"So what'll it be, gov, apple dumplings or rum pudding?" Willy asked, enjoying himself immensely.

Forrest grimaced. "Humble pie, I suppose."

Only one of the other men snickered. The rest were in sympathy for the toff who'd been rolled, horse, boots, and saddle, by a slip of a girl. The brotherhood of man went deeper than class lines.

Wally scratched his head. "You insulted her good this time, gov. She won't be getting over this one half quick."

One of the other footmen called out, "Aw, some

posies're all it'd take. You can see she's daft for 'im."

"Nah," a groom disagreed, spitting tobacco to the side, "she's got half the swells in London sendin' her boo-kets. Ain't I delivered a dozen here myself? It'll take a lot more'n that to win 'er back."

"G'wan, wotta you know? You ain't had a pretty gal smile at you in dog's years. A little slap and tickle, that's all it takes to get 'em eatin' out o' your hands like birds."

"You English, what do you know about *amour*?" the French valet from across the street put in. "It is the sweet words, the pretty compliments a mademoiselle craves."

"But Mischief ain't like other girls."

"What did you say?" Now the viscount was willing to allow a ragtag group of servants to discuss his personal life. At least until his knee stopped throbbing enough for him to walk away without falling on his face. In his current disheveled state, most of the men did not even recognize him. "What did you call her?" he demanded.

Willy answered. "You wouldn't want anybody here using her real name, would you? And we couldn't go calling the bet-recorder 'my lady,' could we? 'Sides, Mischief seemed to fit."

"You don't have to worry, gov," Wally added, "no one here'll squeak beef on her neither, not if they know what's good for them."

The other men were quick to swear their mummers were dubbed. A little gossip in the tap room wasn't worth facing the Minch brothers. 'Sides, Mischief was a real goer, a prime 'un. They wished her the best. If this rumpled cove with the beard-shadowed face was the best, well, she wasn't like other fillies.

Only one of the workingmen in the courtyard did not pledge his silence. This fellow, the same one who snickered before, was edging his way to the rear gate before the viscount took a closer look at the company. Willy saw the bloke creeping away and stopped him with a "Hey, where do you think you're going?"

Wally snagged the little man by the muffler he had wound around his head and neck. The runt made a dash for the gate, leaving his scarf in Wally's hands, but Willy tackled him, sat on him, and punched those rabbity teeth, and a few others, back down his throat. "That was just in case you thought of talking to anybody about any of this," Willy warned. "And it looks better, too."

He tossed Randy over the garden wall like a jar of slops, then wiped his hands.

"Who was that?" Lord Mayne asked.

"Just the driver for that old bat who comes every once in a while. He won't be bothering no one hereabouts again, that's for sure."

The other men lost interest as soon as the squatty fellow went down. They were back to discussing the gentry cove's chances with Mischief and placing bets on the outcome. It was just like White's, Forrest realized, for speculating on another's privacy and gambling on someone else's misfortune. As the debate went on as if he weren't there, Forrest also decided that clothes definitely made the man; he was certainly not getting his usual respect, here in this disheveled rig.

"Oi still say if she wants 'im, it don't matter what

'e does. And if she don't want 'im, it still don't matter what 'e does."

"Nah, Missy's got bottom, she'll give a chap a chance to prove hisself. She won't be fooled by no pretty words 'n trinkets. Man's sincere, she'll know."

"Pshaw, they ain't mind readers, you looby. Gent's got to prove hisself, all right. An' the only way a female's ever been convinced is with a ring."

A hush fell over the enclosed space. Those were serious words, fighting words, church words almost. It was one thing to tease a man when he was bowed and bloodied, but a life sentence? It was bad luck even to talk about. Half the men spit over their right shoulders. The French valet crossed himself. The viscount groaned.

Willy and Wally looked at him and grinned. The viscount did not have to be a mind reader, either, to know what they were thinking. He groaned again. Wouldn't Sydney make one hell of a duchess?

22

The Duchess Decides

Surrender did not come easily to an ex-navy officer. Faced with overwhelming odds, though, the viscount gave up. He did what any brave man would when conditions got so far beyond his control; he sent for his mother. On Bren's behalf.

Now, Lady Mayne may have had the finest network of information gathering outside the War Office, but she was itching for first-hand reconnaissance. She heard all about the encroaching females who were hovering on the edge of scandal, clinging to respectability by her son's fingers and her own name as social passport. She would have believed any tales of Brennan's havey-cavey doings, but Forrest's? Schoolroom chits no better than they ought to be? This she had to see for herself. And she would have done just that, showed up in London bag and baggage two weeks ago . . . if it weren't for that jackass of a duke she was married to.

He never came to her except for Christmas, and

she wouldn't go to him except for coronations. He hated her devotion to her dogs; she hated his absorption in politics. Neither would budge. Now there were higher ideals that could not wait for a royal summons. Now mother love had to supplant pride. Now she was too eager to interfere in her sons' lives to let that whopstraw get in her way.

Her Grace traveled in state. Two coaches carried her, her dogs, her dresser, and a maid. Three more coaches bore every insult she could heap on His Grace's household: her own sheets, towels, and pillows, prepared dishes from her own kitchens, her own butler and footmen, her own houseplants. The fourgon followed with her wardrobe, although she had every intention of charging a fortune in modistes' bills to the twiddlepoop while she was in town.

Lady Mayne planned her journey to a nicety, timing her arrival to coincide with the duke's after-luncheon rest period. The hour of silence was considered sacrosanct in his household, she knew, interrupted on pain of dismissal or dishware. The duke was accustomed to retreat to his study, where he reviewed the morning's meetings and speeches, prepared for the afternoon session, and sometimes took a nap, the old rasher of wind.

Hamilton Mainwaring, Duke of Mayne, was dreaming of the brilliant speech he would give, if he ever kept a secretary long enough to write it. That's when his wife descended on Mainwaring House with her dogs, servants, and trunks. There were servants carrying trunks, servants carrying dogs, servants directing other servants. And more dogs. The duchess couldn't very well leave any home, certainly not Pennyfeather's new puppies.

They were all in the hall, yipping and yapping and tripping over each other and the London staff.

The duke's bellow of outrage warmed the cockles of his lady's heart; the sound of crockery smashing was worth every jolt and rattle of the last hurried miles. His thundering footsteps down the hall brought a smile to her lips as she gaily called out, "Hello, darling, I'm home. Aren't you pleased?"

Hostilities recommenced after tea, when the duke realized his Sondra's visit was not a concession, just a tactical maneuver. He discovered quickly enough that she had not concluded at long last that her place was by her husband's side. She was not staying in London to be his hostess and helpmate, and everything from the dust on the chandeliers to the war with Napoleon was All His Fault.

Brennan recalled a previous engagement. Forrest had calculated his mother's timing even closer than she had. He was out for the day, dining at his club, promised for the evening. No matter, Lady Mayne had not come to see him anyway.

"Then what the devil *are* you here for, madam, if a poor husband may be permitted to ask?"

Lady Mayne made sure the tea things were wheeled out before she told him. She was partial to the Wedgwood. "I am here, husband, because you have made micefeet of my sons' lives."

"I have?" he blustered. "I have, when it's you who keeps them tied to your apron strings? You have Forrest hopping back and forth like some deuced yo-yo, and you won't let Brennan take the colors like every lad dreams of doing. And *I* am ruining their lives?"

"Yes, you. You live here, don't you? You have

eyes to see what is around you, ears to hear that the Mainwaring name is on everybody's lips. And what have you done? Nothing. You are letting your own sons fall into the clutches of penniless nobodies, underbred adventuresses, fortune-hunting hoydens!"

"Well, they ain't nobodies, for one thing. General Lattimore's a fine man, well respected and all that."

"He was a vile-tempered, hard-drinking curmudgeon twenty years ago. I don't fancy he's changed."

The duke cleared his throat. "You can't say they have no breeding either, no matter if it is your hobbyhorse. They are Windhams on the mother's side. Nothing to be ashamed of there."

"Just long noses and a tendency to die early! Thin blood they have, all of them. I met the mother, and a weak, puny thing she was. I was not surprised she cocked up her heels so young. No stamina."

The duke rather thought he recalled Mrs. Lattimore had died in a carriage accident; he was too cagey a fish to be drawn to that fly, though, and too relieved. "So you really do know the family. I couldn't imagine why the boy put it about that you had an interest there."

The duchess pursed her lips. "Couldn't you? He was thinking with his inexpressibles, that's why. The little climbers must have put him up to it, to smooth their way up the social ladder. I met the mother once, as I said. Elizabeth Windham was much younger, don't you know, and we were traveling then. My cousin Trevor was bowled over by her. She had that fragile beauty men seem to admire. But Elizabeth tossed him over for a uniform, ran off with young Lattimore and broke my cousin's heart. He died soon after, so I ain't likely to take her chicks under my wing."

The duke knew for a fact Trevor died of a weakness of the lungs. That's when Sondra started wrapping her own boys in cotton. He was not about to mention that tidbit either, having learned early on that facts only slowed his lady's flow of thought, never diverted it or dammed it. "Well, I don't think you need worry about them hanging on your sleeves. That Harriet Windham's managed to get them on all the right guest lists."

"I always supposed that nipcheese was behind this whole thing, trying to snabble rich husbands for her nieces. Heaven knows what she hopes to do for her own whey-faced chit, but she's not going to snag my sons!"

"I hear the elder Miss Lattimore is a real beauty," the duke offered.

His lady waved that aside. "I hope a Mainwaring has too much sense to fall for a pretty face. Those empty-headed belles make poor—what do you mean, you *hear* she's a beauty? Haven't you seen her for yourself, this harpy with her claws in your own son? Didn't you care sufficiently to take your head out of that dreary office long enough to check, you pettifogging excuse for a father?"

"I care, blast it, I care!" The duke was shouting, growing red in the face.

The duchess ran to the mantel and handed him the ormolu clock there. "Here, throw this," she said. "Your aunt Lydia sent it as a wedding gift. I always hated it."

The duke carefully placed the ornate thing back in its spot. "I know, that's why I always kept it."

Then he turned to her and grinned. "Ah, Sondra, my sunshine, how I have missed you."

The duchess colored prettily, and at her age! "Sussex is not so far away, you know."

"But would I find welcome there, or would a dog be sleeping in my bed like last time, when I had to take a guest room?"

"Are you trying to change the subject, Hamilton? It won't wash. What about the boys?"

"Dash it, Sondra, they are men, not boys, and I do care. I care enough to let them make their own mistakes, the same way we did."

"And look where it got us!" she retorted.

"I am," was all he said, and she was glad she had on her new lilac gown, the way he was staring at her with that special gleam in his eye.

"Humph! First we'll see about those upstarts, then we'll see about *that*."

The duchess took her battle to the enemy camp. The duke hurried out to buy a new corset.

Lady Mayne was not surprised to find Harriet Windham at the Lattimores' for tea, she was only surprised how much she still disliked the woman after all these years. Trust that lickpenny to eat anyone else's food but her own and to thrust her own fubsy daughter into a prettier girl's orbit. The duchess could not like how Lady Windham rushed to greet her at the door, neatly stepping in front of the pretty gal and pinching the other chit when she started to say something. Now the toadeater was ordering the Misses Lattimore to tend to less noble guests, including the duchess's son Brennan, while Harriet fawned over the most exalted. Gads, if she had wanted a chat with the squeeze-farthing, Her

Grace would have called at Windham House, not Park Lane. And she would have eaten more first. The almond tarts she was generously being offered here—by the daughters of the house, not servants, she noted—were quite good.

She delicately wiped a crumb from her lip and fired her first salvo: "My dear Harriet, I know it has been ages, but you must not let me keep you from the rest of your calls."

"Don't think anything of it, Your Grace. Beatrix and I have nowhere better—"

Second round: "I am sure. I would like to get to know Elizabeth's charming daughters, however."

"How kind you are to take an interest. Perhaps I should plan a dinner—"

The broadside: "Alone. Now."

Brennan came to her side after the Windhams left. "Masterful, Your Grace," he applauded. "May I stay, or am I *de trop* also?"

"You may bring me that attractive young woman you were drooling over, then take yourself off."

"Attractive? Mother, she's the most beautiful girl in the world. And the sweetest. And just wait till you see her on a horse."

"What, that porcelain doll?"

Bren grinned, reminding her of his father when they met. "She's naught but a country girl, Mother. She knows all about flowers and things. I can't wait to show her your gardens at the Chance, and see what she thinks about that old property of Uncle Homer's." The duchess sighed. She was too late.

She was also delighted with Winifred, who truly was as lovely as she was pretty. She was unspoiled and unaffected, only slightly in awe of meeting Bren's august parent. This last impressed the duchess most, for she remembered her first meeting with the dowager. Her knees might show bruises to this day from knocking together so hard. Lady Mayne also noted how Winifred kept looking to make sure the other sister took care of the general and the rest of the company. If her conversation wasn't brilliant, well, even his doting mother never considered Brennan a mental giant. Incredible as it seemed, the chawbacon seemed to have found himself a pearl. And without his mother's help. She waved the chit off to save him from a boring conversation with a Tulip in a bottle-green suit.

Before the duchess could spot her next quarry, the girl was curtsying to her, and winking! "Did she pass muster, Your Grace?" the brazen young woman was asking with a grin that showed perfect dimples under dancing eyes and curls that—ah, so that explained the bundle her son carried from place to place. Well, it did not really, so the duchess asked.

"My, ah, hair? I am sorry, Your Grace, but I really cannot explain that. I mean, I could, but I don't think I should. I was somewhere I should not have been and Lord Mayne—the viscount, that is, not the duke—was there, too. And he helped. Oh, but you mustn't think poorly of him for being there or, or for acting not quite the gentleman. About the hair, that is."

Not quite the gentleman, her oh-so-proper son Forrest? The duchess was intrigued by the girl's artlessness, and how she did not even seem aware that she was under scrutiny the same as her sister. "My dear," the duchess said, patting her hand, "you have been without a mother too long if you think I could believe ill of my son. It is always some other mother's progeny who is to blame."

Sydney grinned again. "Do you know, your son feels the same way! Whenever he gets himself in a snit or a fit of the sullens, it always seems to be my fault."

Tempers? Moods? The duchess wondered if they were speaking of the same person. Forrest was the most unprovokable man of her experience, and she had been trying for years. Oh, this was a chit after her own heart. "Miss Lattimore, do you like dogs?"

The duchess returned home to inform the duke that he'd done just what he ought, and found their sons the perfect brides.

"Brilliant, my dear, brilliant," she congratulated him over their pre-dinner sherry.

"I thought they didn't have a feather to fly with."

"Pooh, who's talking about money? Of course nothing's settled yet, so I might have to stay on in town to take a hand in matters after all."

The duke pretended to study his ancestor's portrait on the wall. "Might you, my dear?"

"Of course, I would need an escort sometimes, you know, to show we both countenanced the match. If that would not pull you away from your duties terribly."

His Grace tossed back his wine and held out his arm to lead her in to dinner. "Family support is worth the sacrifice. You can count on me, my dear," he said with a bow. His new corsets creaked only a little.

23

Miss Lattimore . . . or Less

*V*iscount Mayne did not usually peek into the breakfast room before entering, but with the duchess in town, forewarned was forearmed. He'd rather go without his kippers and eggs than have his hair combed with a bowl of porridge so early in the morning. The duchess was smiling, though, and humming over her chocolate and some lists she was writing. He entered, careful to watch for the furry little beggars one always found lapping up crumbs in Her Grace's breakfast parlor.

"Good morning, Mother," he said, dropping a kiss on her bent head before helping himself at the sideboard. "I see you are keeping country hours. Did you sleep well or did the London noise awaken you?"

Oddly, she blushed. "I slept very well, thank you. I wished to speak with your father this morning before he left for his office." The viscount looked around for pottery shards. "And you before you went on your usual ride." Or escape hatches.

"I think I'll just send for some fresh coffee," he said, moving to the bellpull.

"It's fresh, dearest. And so are the eggs, done just the way you like them. Sit. Oh, no, Forrest, I did not mean you. Pumpkin was trying to steal Prince Charlie's bacon."

Forrest excused himself. He was not particularly hungry any longer.

"But you cannot go until we've talked about my dinner party."

"Are you staying in town long enough to throw a party, then? Father will be pleased." He hoped so. He himself was planning on being busy that night, whichever night she chose. Lady Mayne's London circle was the worst bunch of character assassins he ever met, meddlers and intriguers all. Now that the duchess was in London to look after Bren, perhaps Forrest could return to the peace and quiet of the countryside.

"Yes, I thought I would host a small gathering to introduce Miss Lattimore to our closest friends."

He sat down in a hurry. Sydney at the mercy of those gossipmongers? Heaven knew what she would do if he wasn't there to look after her. "Brennan told me you visited at Park Lane. So you mean to take them up?"

The duchess looked up from her lists. "Of course. That's what you intended when you wrote me, wasn't it? They'd be quite ruined if I were to cut the connection now, after the mull you made of introducing them. A friend of their mother's, indeed! Lucky for you I even knew the peahen."

Forrest waved that aside. "Then you don't mind that Miss Lattimore hasn't a feather to fly with?"

Lady Mayne set down her pencil. "I hope I have

not raised my sons to think that money can buy happiness, for it cannot. Then, too, Brennan shall have an adequate income to provide for any number of wives."

"And their families. You don't think they could be fortune hunters, do you?"

"Stuff and nonsense. How could you look at that sweet girl and stay so cynical?" She frowned at him as if the idea never entered her mind. "I think she and her sister have done the best they could to keep themselves above oars, considering all the help they got from that cheeseparing aunt. Why, she has a houseful of underpaid servants, and her own nieces fetch and carry like maids. She must have a barn full of equipages, and they travel about in hired carriages! It's the outside of enough, and I have already taken steps to see things changed. See how Lady Windham likes the ton knowing a near stranger has to frank her relations. The duke agrees."

Forrest choked on a piece of toast. Now, that was a first, the Mainwarings agreeing about anything. Forrest could not help wondering how Sydney felt about his mother's largess, with her prickly pride.

"I was *not* high-handed, Forrest. I let Bren manage it. She's his intended, after all."

"And you are reconciled to the match even though it is not a brilliant one?"

"Who says it is not? She is going to keep him happy and safe at home. What more could I want? And can you imagine what beautiful children they will have? I cannot wait to see if they are dark like Brennan or fair like Winifred."

Forrest had a second helping of eggs. "I am relieved you found her so charming, Mother. I thought you would."

"Yes, and I don't even mind that she is an independent thinker and an original, either."

"Independent? Winnie? If the girl had two thoughts to rub together, I never heard them."

"Who said I was talking about Miss Lattimore? I am speaking of your Miss Sydney, who does not have more hair than wit. And if you did not send for me to get your ducks in a row with that refreshing young miss, I'll eat my best bonnet."

"She's not refreshing, she's exhausting. She is a walking disaster who is forever on the verge of some scandal. *That's* why I sent for you, before she could ruin Winnie's chances, too. Sydney is infuriating and devious and always up to her pretty little neck in mischief."

"Yes, dear," his mother said, bending over her lists, "that's why you are top-over-trees in love with her."

The fork hit the plate. "Me? In love with Sydney? Fustian! Who said anything about love? She's a wild young filly who will never be broke to bridle, and I am too old to try."

"Of course. That's why you carry her hair from London to Sussex and back again."

The viscount couldn't keep his eyes from flashing upward. "Never tell me you check my rooms, Your Grace."

"I didn't have to, dear. You just told me."

"I thought the hair upset you at the manor," he said, praying that the warmth he felt was not showing as red on his face. "That's all there is to it, by George."

"Don't swear, Forrest. You've been around your

father too much. And don't worry over being so blind you cannot recognize what your own heart is telling you. Your father never believed he loved me either until I told him. Just don't wait too long, Forrest, for royalty won't be too high for Miss Sydney when I am through."

The coffee was bitter and the eggs were cold. Forrest put his plate on the floor for the dogs to squabble over and excused himself. "I am sure you and the housekeeper can work out all the details for your dinner party. Father's new secretary seems a capable sort, too, but feel free to call on me if I can be of assistance."

She was back at her lists before he reached the door. "Oh, by the way, Forrest," she called when his hand touched the knob, "I gave Sydney a dog."

The viscount's hand fell to his side and his head struck the door. "Do you really hate me that much, Mother?"

Did he love her? Not which horse should he ride, which route should he take to the park, just: Did he love her? Forrest controlled his mount through the traffic, galloped down the usual rides, cooled the chestnut gelding on tree-shaded pathways, all without noticing the other men also exercising their cattle or the nursemaids with their charges or the old ladies feeding the pigeons. He was lost in the center of London, lost in his thoughts.

He supposed he did love her. He surely had all the attics-to-let symptoms of a mooncalf in love. But could he live with Sydney Lattimore? Hell, could he live without her?

He had yet another concern: Did she love him? He knew from her kisses that she was not altogether unresponsive to him, but she also resented him, sometimes despised him, and never respected him. More often than not, she looked at him as if he were queerer than Dick's hatband. Maybe he was, to care what she thought. Hang it, he'd had more kicks than kisses from the wench!

His mother thought Sydney loved him, for what the opinion of another totty-headed, illogical female was worth. Plenty, most likely, he thought as he picked up the horse's pace again. Now, there was another woman he never hoped to understand. The duke said you'd end up crosseyed if you tried, anyway. But the duchess had always preached propriety, breeding, duty to the family name. Now she was pleased to consider one of the devil's own imps as her successor. He shuddered at the thought. Sydney as duchess meant Sydney as his wife.

Confused by the mixed signals it was receiving, the chestnut reared. Forrest brought it back under control with a firm hand and a pat on the neck. "Sorry, old fellow. My fault for wool-gathering. I don't suppose you have any advice?" The horse shook its head and resumed the canter. "No, gelding is not the answer."

He set his mind to the matter at hand, looking out for other riders and strollers now that the park was getting more crowded. When they reached another shaded alleyway, however, Forrest let the horse pick their way while he searched his mind for answers.

If he loved Sydney, he should marry her. If she loved him, she would marry him. He did not think for a moment that she would wed for convenience, not his Sydney with her fiery emotions. And there was no longer a reason for her to make a cream-pot marriage, not with Winnie's future guaranteed. She had to know Brennan would look after her, and the general as well. Forrest would see to the settlements himself, ensuring she never had to concoct any more bubble-headed schemes, even if she did not marry him.

But she would marry him if she loved him. If he asked. Zeus, what if she refused? What if a slip of a girl with less sense than God gave a duck refused the Viscount of Mayne, one of the most eligible bachelors in London? He'd never recover, that's what. She'd be a fool to turn down his title, wealth, and prospects, but he would be shattered.

And the duchess would know. She always did. Gads, he'd have to listen to her taunts whenever he was at home, unless she told all her friends. Then he'd be a laughingstock everywhere he went. He may as well move to the Colonies, for all the joy he'd find in England.

He reined the horse to a standstill, tipping his hat to a family of geese crossing the path to the Serpentine. The gossip did not matter any more than the honking of the geese. There would be no joy without Sydney, period.

Such being the case, he acknowledged, kneeing the horse onward, still at a walk, there was nothing for it but to put his luck to the touch. He had to ask. But when? His mother had both girls so hedged about with callers and servants, he'd never get to see Sydney alone now. The duchess was not leaving the rumor hounds a whiff of scandal. Forrest was glad, for no one with baser desires could reach the Lattimores either. He had not forgotten about the moneylending scum and still had men watching the house and scouring London for Randall and Chester. His men had turned up the information that they were brothers, as unlikely as it seemed, by the name of O'Toole. Bow Street was also extremely interested in their whereabouts.

Let Bow Street worry about the blackguards, Forrest decided. The best way to keep Sydney safe was to keep her by his side. Which, he thought with a frown, his own mother was preventing. He might get her alone the night of the betrothal dinner his mother was hosting for Brennan and Winifred. He could suggest showing Sydney the family portrait gallery. No, he would feel all those eyes were watching him play the fool. Perhaps a visit to the jade collection in the Adams Room, he mused. No, the locked cabinets reminded him of his parents' stormy relationship.

As he went on a mental tour of Mainwaring House, the viscount discovered a new romantical quirk to his thinking. He wanted Sydney where no one could disturb them, in daylight when he could see the emotions flicker in her hazel eyes. He wanted to ask her to live with him at Mayne Chance, *at* Mayne Chance.

They were all coming to Sussex for the holidays, after the Season. The wedding would be held there after the new year, he understood from Bren, in the family chapel.

Yes, the Chance was the perfect place to take his own chance. The holidays added a special excitement anyway, with parties throughout the neighborhood, mistletoe, kissing boughs, and the whole castle decorated in greenery. With excursions to gather the holly and the yule log, to deliver baskets to the tenants and flowers to the church, he would surely find the ideal opportunity. Maybe there would be snow, with sleigh rides, long walks, ice skating, and snowball fights with his sisters' children. Forrest found he couldn't wait to show Sydney his home, his heritage, her future.

His mother was wrong; there was no rush. Forrest could wait for the perfect time, the perfect place. He smiled and set the gelding to a measured trot. "Time to go home, boy."

Suddenly his mount reared. Then it bucked and crow-hopped and tossed its head. Forrest managed to stay on by sheer luck and ingrained good horsemanship, for he hadn't been paying attention this time either, visions of Sydney with snowflakes falling on rosy cheeks obscuring his view of Rotten Row.

He collected the Thoroughbred and was straightening his disordered neckcloth when he noticed that the chestnut had flecks of blood on its head. Holding the reins firmly, Forrest dismounted.

"What the deuce?" The gelding's ear appeared to have a clean slice partway through. Forrest looked around and saw no one. Still holding the reins, he murmured soothing words to the horse and led it back to where his beaver hat lay on the path. He kept looking behind him, in the trees, through the shrubbery. Damn, there were a million places an ambusher could hide. Then his eye caught the glint of metal and he tugged the still-nervous animal off the tanbark. A knife was embedded in a tree trunk at just about the height of his head when astride. "Hell and damnation," he cursed under his breath at his own stupidity.

Figuring the assailant to be long gone, Forrest pocketed the knife and remounted. He retraced their path, keeping his wits about him this time.

The only person he saw was a bent old woman with a cane and a shawl over her head, sitting on a stone bench. A flock of pigeons pecked at the grass near her feet.

"Good day, Grandmother," the viscount called. "Did you see anyone come after me on the path?"

The old hag raised her head. "Whatch that, sonny?" she asked through bare gums, her mouth caved in around missing teeth.

"I said, did you see someone following me? Anybody suspicious?"

"No, and no." The crone shook her head sadly. "M'eyesight ain't what it used to be."

Forrest tossed her a coin and rode away. The old woman cursed and tore the shawl off her head, leaving a crop of red hair. Then she threw her spectacles on the ground and jumped on them. Then she kicked a pigeon or two. Randy hadn't listened to his mother either.

24

Sydney and Sensibilities

Something was wrong. Circumstances were at their best, yet Sydney felt her worst. She was thrilled at Winifred's good fortune, truly she was. Winnie's slippers had not touched the ground since the duchess nodded her approval. Sydney's sister would be wrapped round with love and happiness, tied with a golden future like the most wonderful, glittering Christmas gift. And Sydney was not satisfied.

They had no more worries about squeezing the general's pension so hard it cried, and Sydney's own dowry was to be restored with all debts—unspecified—absorbed under the terms of the settlements. Sydney and the general were invited to make their homes with Bren and Winnie in Hampshire when they went, or with the duke and duchess in London and Sussex. So there was nothing to get in a pother about.

But it wasn't enough, Sydney knew. She did not want to be a charity case, even if she were the only one who considered herself in that light. She did not want to be a poor relation, hanging on her sister's coattails, the bridesmaid going along on the honeymoon. As much as she liked and admired the duchess, she did not think she would be happy in another woman's household either, especially not one where the china had an uncertain future and the eldest son was likely to bring home a bride of his own at any time. No, she would not think of that.

What she did think of, what kept her chewing on her lip, was that she had not met her goals. She had not satisfied her honor. With the best of intentions and far better results than she could have attained, the Mainwarings were taking over her responsibilities. They were making decisions for her, providing for her, caring for her. She even rode in one of their carriages. Sydney was back to being the little sister, and she did not care for it one whit.

There was a big hole in her life, not filled by all the picnics and parties and fittings and fussing over clothes the duchess insisted on, nor by the maids and grooms and errand boys the duchess deemed necessary for Winnie's consequence. The hole was where her plans and schemes, daydreams and fancies, used to occupy her thoughts. She used to feel excitement, anticipation, the sense that she was doing something worthwhile, something for herself and her loved ones. Now she felt . . . nothing.

There was a bigger emptiness in her heart. He never came except on polite, twenty-minute calls with his mother. He never asked for more than one dance at any of the balls, and he never held her hand longer than necessary. He no longer ordered her about, threatened her, or shouted at her. He did not curse or call her names, and he never, ever made her indecent proposals.

Sydney did not really expect Forrest to continue his atrocious behavior, not with all the maids and chaperones the duchess stacked like a fence around her and Winnie's virtue. And she did not really expect him to repeat his outrageous offer, not with his mother in town.

Well, yes, she did. He was a rake, and no rake would let a few old aunties or abigails get in his way. He'd never been bothered about speaking his mind in front of Willy or Wally. And no rake in any of the Minerva Press romances ever even *had* a mother, much less pussyfooted around her feelings. The duchess said he was dull and always had been. Sydney knew better. He just didn't care anymore.

So Sydney wouldn't care either, so there. It did not matter anyway, she told herself; her dog loved her. Princess Pennyfleur was a delight. Sydney called her Puff for short, since all of the Duchess's Princess dogs answered to Penny, and Puff was so special she deserved a name of her own. The little dog was always happy, wearing that silly Pekingese grin that made Sydney smile. She was always ready to romp and play or go for a walk, or just sit quietly next to Sydney while she read. Puff wasn't like any unreliable male, blowing hot, then cold.

Even the general enjoyed the little dog. He held her in his lap, stroking her silky head for hours when Sydney was out in the evenings. Griffith thought the general's hand was growing stronger from all the exercise. Puff was wise enough to jump down if the general grew agitated, before he started pounding on anything.

They made quite a stir in the park, too, just as

the duchess predicted. Traffic at the fashionable hour came to a halt when Sydney walked by with her coppery curls and her matching dog curled like a muff in her arms or trotting at her heels. It was a picture for Lawrence or Reynolds, or Bella Bumpers.

"We gotta nab her in the park. It's the only place she ain't cheek-to-jowls with an army of flunkies. She don't have time for me no more, and they've got a carriage of their own now, not that she would get back into the carriage after that time with you at the reins, Fido."

Randy had a new set of teeth. Actually, he had half of a new set, the bottoms. These ivories, from a blacksmith who had been kicked in the mouth once too often, were again too big for Randy, so his lower jaw jutted out over the upper, giving him the appearance of a bulldog. He blamed the viscount for that, too, setting Bow Street on their tail. Now neither of the brothers dared show his own face outdoors long enough for Randy to visit a real denturemaker. He never admitted to Bella that the footmen smashed the first set, not the viscount, so the grudge was a heavier weight on her back, too.

They were holding their latest planning session in the basement at their house in Chelsea, the only place Chester felt secure.

"I'm not going to do it, Mama," he whimpered now. "It's not safe. We've got to get out of London. To hell with the money, I say."

"You'd say you were mad King George if you thought it would save your skin, pigeon-heart. 'Sides, we're all packed. We just have to snag the gel and catch the packet at Dover. We'll have it all.

First he'll pay, then we give out her suicide note saying he ruined her. He'll be finished. It's perfect."

Chester lost what color he had. "We're not going to kill the girl, Mama. You promised."

"Nah, Chester, we're going to let the wench swim back to England and fit us for hemp neckties." Randy was practicing his knife-throwing. One landed a shiver's distance from Chester's foot.

"I'm not going, then. I'm not having anything to do with murder. Mayne would find us at the ends of the earth. Besides, she's seen me too many times. The footman, then that fellow Chesterton. She'll recognize me for sure. It won't work. I won't— yeow!"

Chester was going, only now he'd limp.

Leaves crunching under her feet, not even Sydney could be in the doldrums on such a pretty fall day. She had on a forest-green pelisse with the hood up, with Puff on a green ribbon leash scampering at her side. Brennan and Winnie walked just ahead, since there was room for only two abreast on this less frequented path they chose. Sydney slowed her steps to give them some quiet time alone. They must be feeling the lack of privacy even more than she was.

Wally and Annemarie followed after, but they were discussing their own futures. If the Minch brothers stayed with Sydney and the general, how could Annemarie go off to Hampshire with Winifred? But it was a better position, and Wally might never be able to afford that inn, or a wife. No one would arm-wrestle with him anymore, and he'd promised his mother, Sydney, and Annemarie not to enter another prizefight. So involved were they in their conversation, and the pretty maid's anguish which needed to be assuaged behind a concealing tree, that they did not notice Sydney was no longer with her sister and Lord Mainwaring. She could have been beaten, drugged, and stuffed in a sack before they noticed she was gone, which was Bella's intention, except for the sack.

"Help, miss, oh, help!" the bent old woman cried as she used her cane to clear a way through some bushes to the path where Sydney walked. "We've been set on by footpads! My little girl is hurt! Oh, help!" She grabbed on to Sydney's arm with a surprisingly strong grip for one so ancient and frail, and tried to drag her back off the path with her. "My Chessie, my baby. Oh, please come help, kind lady."

The woman had an overbite like Puff's, though not as attractive, and bits of red hair sticking out from her turban. Her voice was a shrill whisper of distress.

"I'll get my footman, ma'am; he'll send for the watch," Sydney offered, trying to turn back.

"Mama," came a screeching falsetto from behind the bushes.

"They're long gone," the old lady told her, pulling Sydney forward. "And I just need you to help me get my little girl Chessie back to the coach. Do you have any vinaigrette? Hartshorn?"

"No, but my maid is right behind me. She must have something." Sydney looked back, wondering just where Annemarie and Wally were. She knew she should not get out of their sight, but a lady in such dire straits . . .

"Don't worry, dear, I'm Mrs. Otis. Everyone knows

me. Your maid will find you, but we can have poor Chessie in the carriage by then. It's her foot, you see."

And indeed another female was limping toward them, crying into a large handkerchief. Her cheeks looked rouged and her dress was not quite the thing either, being a coliquet-striped silk with cherry ribbons. The female's hair, under a bonnet with three ostrich feathers, was an improbable yellow shade. All in all, Sydney realized this was not a person she should know.

The outfit had not been to Chester's taste either, but Bella's short, wide black dresses did not fit his tall, thin frame, and he was not about to go outside to shop the second-hand stalls. The only business next door this week was a Covent Garden streetwalker who'd died of the French disease. The mortician swore on his mother's grave Chester couldn't catch the pox by wearing her dress. Of course the mortician's mother didn't have a grave; he'd sold her body to the anatomy college. Chester did not know that, so he stuffed some more stockings in the bodice, crying the whole time anyway. He limped effectively, too, with his weight on Sydney so she had to keep moving toward the coach she saw ahead.

"But, but it's a hearse!" Sydney exclaimed when she got a better look at the vehicle with its black curtains, black horses, and casket sticking out of the back.

"Yes, isn't it a shame?" the old woman lamented. "Here we are, on our way to bury Chessie's husband, and she felt the need to get out and compose herself in the serenity of nature. Then what should happen but three ruffians jumped on us! They robbed the money to pay the grave diggers, can you imagine? Then they knocked down poor Chessie and stole her wedding ring. What is this world coming to?"

Sydney didn't know, when the driver with his black top hat and weepers didn't get down to help two women in obvious distress, and when a bereft wife dressed more like bachelor fare than grieving widow. "What is this world coming to, indeed?" she echoed.

By the time they finally reached the carriage, Sydney was breathing hard. Mrs. Otis opened the door and stood back for Sydney to help Chessie up . . . with the weighted handle of her cane poised near Sydney's head. The coffin lid creaked open a crack so Bella could breathe inside it without being knocked out by the ether-dipped cloth in her hand. And Chessie wept. Sydney put one foot on the carriage steps and hauled Chessie up. Then a dog barked.

"Puff!" Sydney shouted. "I forget all about my little dog! Here, Puff, here I am." She pushed right past the unprepared Mrs. Otis, leaving Chester to teeter on the steps. They could hear the dog barking and, getting closer, Wally's voice calling "Miss Sydney." Brennan Mainwaring shouted from the other direction.

Chester couldn't catch her, not with his foot bandaged like a mummy, and Bella couldn't get out of the coffin in time. Randy bent to throw the knife in his boot, then recalled he wasn't wearing boots. "Bloody hell," Randy cursed, "let's get out of here." So he shoved Chester through the door, smack into the ether-sopped rag, and sprang in after him. Bella pushed the coffin lid aside, hard, right through Randy's new choppers. The coach was already moving.

When Sydney brought her friends back to the clearing to see if they could be of further assistance, no one and nothing was there, except some ivory dentures Puff found. Bottoms.

25

Plans and Provisions

The duchess could well understand Sydney's me-
grims. Forrest's intransigence was enough to make
a saint blue-deviled. Lady Mayne asked him over
and over, and all the close-mouthed churl answered
was that the time wasn't right. Stuff, he'd be cutting up chickens and consulting stargazers next.
What was worse, she could not even discuss it with
Sydney to reassure the poor girl. The duchess didn't
want to get the lass's hopes up, in case her war-
hero son never gathered enough courage to come
up to scratch. Moreover, the duke threatened mayhem if she meddled. With all their friends coming
to dinner in two weeks, she could not chance the
monogrammed dishes.

Then there was the matter of that loan, the one
not spelled out in the settlements. The duke vowed
he knew nothing about it, and Forrest was as quiet
as a clam. It would have been beyond the pale to
question Sydney, and useless to subject Bren to an
inquisition, for he was more in awe of his brother

than of his mother. But the duchess knew about the hair and she knew about pride, better than most.

"You know, Sydney," she casually remarked as they wrote out invitations one afternoon, "it occurred to me that you might think me an interfering old biddy, sending you servants, ordering your life about."

"Never, Your Grace." Sydney jumped up to get more cards to address and kissed the older woman's cheek. "Aunt Harriet is an interfering old biddy, you are an interfering old dear. You are kind and generous and have only Winifred's best interests at heart. I would be cloddish in the extreme not to be grateful."

"Yes, but gratitude can be wearing on one," the duchess persisted. "I do not want you to feel the least bit indebted, especially not to my son."

"I shall always be thankful to Lord Mainwaring for the care he takes of Winnie and the general," Sydney answered hesitantly, not sure she liked the trend of this conversation. The duchess was charming, and as sneaky as she could dare.

"I didn't mean Brennan, my dear."

"Did he tell you? That villain! He swore the loan was forgotten, that he wouldn't take the money back under any conditions! Why, I'll—"

The duchess moved the ink pot, from long practice. "No, my dear, Forrest would never be so ungentlemanly." Ignoring the snort of derision from her young friend, she went on. "You must know Forrest would not go back on his word. No, I just got a hint of a loan, from little snippets of information. And no, I am not prying into the details. Of course, if you should wish to confide in me . . . No, well, as I was saying, I do not wish to intrude, but I cannot help noticing a degree of constraint between you two. I would not wish you to be—" She almost started to say that she did not wish Sydney and Forrest to begin their married life with a mole-hill between them; marriage provided enough mountains to climb. She caught herself in time. "I do not wish you two proud people to be at odds."

Sydney laughed. "I suppose I do have a surfeit of pride, Your Grace, for I should dearly love to pay him back, but I could never find the money and he would never take it. For that matter, I would love to throw a ball for Winnie's engagement, to repay all the hostesses who have invited us throughout the Season, and I cannot do that either. I thought Aunt Harriet might, being the bride's family and all." Now it was Her Grace's turn to make rude noises. "But Winnie does not mind, so I shall have to swallow more of my damnable pride. And please," she said before the duchess could say anything, "do *not* offer me the funds, because then I would be offended."

"You wouldn't let me . . . ?"

"You have already done so much, why, I wish I could do something for you!"

"You can, dear girl, you can." You can shake my stodgy son from his cave of complacency, she thought, and out into the sunshine and moonlight.

The duchess had a plan, a great and glorious plan, making Sydney's schemes look like child's play. Best of all, the enterprise was neither dangerous, scandalous, nor illegal. It was perfect. Sydney was going to throw a ball!

"But, ma'am, you cannot have thought. The money, the space, all the expenses . . ."

"Stuff and nonsense, child, think. We're both country girls, so tell me: If the church needs a new roof, what do the parishioners do?"

Sydney giggled. "They dun the richest man in the neighborhood. Is that what I should do?"

"Don't be impertinent, miss. If the local nabob does not choose to buy his place in heaven, what then? What if a farmer's barn burns down? Don't tell me things are so different in Little Dedham. Now use that pretty brain box of yours."

"Why, the villagers would all donate what they could to the church, and they would all get together to help rebuild the barn. Sometimes they would hold a potluck supper, or an auction to raise money. And sometimes," Sydney said, excitement building in her voice, "they would throw a subscription dance, where everyone paid an entry fee and the money went to charity!"

"Exactly! We'll make the guests pay for the pleasure of your ball."

"But that's countryfolk," Sydney said uncertainly. "Not the quality here in London."

"Fustian. Pick a worthy charity and they'll come. There's nothing the wealthy like better than getting something back for their money. You'll help them feel generous without getting their hands dirty. That way you can reciprocate your invitations and show off your sister with all the pomp and glory you want."

The pride of the Lattimores, Sydney thought fondly, but they could never afford it.

"Goose, you tell the guests beforehand that the *profits* are going to a good cause, so they know the expenses are being deducted. You don't need much for the original outlay; most merchants are used to getting paid months later. I shall underwrite the refreshments, and I'll take great pleasure in seeing that Lady Windham pays for the orchestra. I'd make her pay for the food, but I fear we'd be served only tea and toast."

Sydney was laughing now; it really was fun to let one's daydreams take flight, even if they could never come home to roost. "Your Grace, I am sorry to disappoint you when your scheme is so lovely, but there is not even a ballroom in the house. Indeed, our whole house could fit in some ballrooms I've seen. And if we hold the ball at Mainwaring House, as I can see you are going to suggest, then it will not be the Lattimore ball."

"No such thing. We'll hire the Argyle Rooms. They cannot say no if it's for charity. And I'll make sure we get a deuced good price, too."

Sydney thought a good many people must find it hard to say no to the duchess. Out loud she voiced more objections. The duchess had an answer for each.

"Flowers are very expensive."

"So we'll call it a holly ball. There's acres of the stuff growing at Mayne Chance, and armies of gardeners doing nothing this time of year. You'll have to make arrangements out of the stuff, of course, you and Winifred and that platter-faced cousin of yours. Everyone will have a share of the expenses, a share of the work."

"You're forgetting that Winnie and I are just young girls. I never heard of two females hosting a ball."

"I do not forget anything but my birthday, Sydney. And you are forgetting the general. About time the ton honored one of its heroes. Lattimore will be the host. Be good for the old codger to get out more anyway. Now, what else are you going to nitpick over?"

Sydney had a hard time putting her last objection into words without insulting the duchess. "The, ah, worthy cause, and the, uh, loan from the Viscount of Mayne. You weren't thinking that I should tell everyone the ball was for charity, and then give him the money, were you?"

"Lud, infant, where do you get your notions? You know Forrest won't take your money. He certainly won't take money out of the mouths of babes, or whatever. But if you were to give the money in his name, say, or let him give it to that veterans' group he supports, then I daresay he'd be proud to accept."

And Sydney dared hope he'd smile at her again.

Sydney refused to go one step further with the plans until she consulted the viscount, even if she had to suffer Lady Mayne's knowing looks.

"It's not that I care so much for his approval," she lied, blushing. "I need to confirm which charity he prefers."

So that evening at the Conklins' ball, during their one dance, a waltz, Sydney waited for the usual empty pleasantries to pass. She was looking lovely; he was feeling well. He did not say that she looked like a dancing flame in her gold gown, that her warmth kindled his blood. She did not mention that she thought him the most handsome man she'd ever seen in his formal clothes, that she blushed to think of him out of them.

She appreciated last night's opera; he enjoyed his morning ride. Neither said how much they wished the other had been there to share the pleasure. They danced at just the proper distance apart, in spite of their bodies' aching to touch. They kept the proper social smiles on their faces. Until Sydney mentioned money.

"My lord," Sydney began.

"Forrest."

She nodded. "My lord Forrest, I have been thinking about the thousand pounds you lent me."

His hand tightened on her fingers and closed on her waist. Trying to maintain a smile with his teeth clenched, the viscount ground out, "Don't."

"But your mother agrees with me."

For the first time in ten years the viscount missed his step and trod on his partner's toes. "Sorry." Then Sydney found herself being twirled and swirled across the dance floor and right out the balcony doors. Forrest led her to the farthest, darkest corner. With any luck no one would find her body until the servants came to clean up in the morning.

"You haven't even heard our idea," Sydney complained as his fearsome grip moved to her shoulders. She was glad the shadows hid his scowl.

"Ma'am, every time you get an idea in that pretty little head of yours, I am slapped or kicked or beaten or poisoned. I am always out of pocket and out of temper. Add my mother into the brew and I may as well stick my spoon in the wall now." But his fingers had relaxed on her shoulders. Actually he was now caressing her skin where the gold tissue gown left her bare, almost as if he were unaware of what his fingers were doing. Sydney was very aware.

Her breath coming faster than her thoughts, she stumbled through an explanation of the ball. Farmers' roofs and family pride mixed with wine-merchants' bills and Winifred's betrothal. "But it's really for you, Forrest, so I can give you the money and you can give it to a noble cause. What do you think?"

"I think," he said, pulling her to his chest, where she filled his arms perfectly, "that you are the most impossible, pig-headed, pea-brained female of my experience. And the most wonderful."

He moved to tip her chin up for his kiss, but she was already raising her face toward him in answer, an answer to all of his questions.

Just as their lips were a breath apart, someone coughed loudly. Forrest was tired of watching her glide around with every fop and sweaty-palmed sprig. No more. She was his and he was not going to give her up, not even for a dance. He turned to scare the insolent puppy away. The fellow could come back in a year or two, maybe.

The insolent puppy, however, was the Duke of Mayne, and he was grinning. Forrest decided he liked his father better when he stayed in his office.

"I've come for my dance with the prettiest gal here," the duke declared, winking at Sydney.

She chuckled softly, reaching up to straighten the tiara of daisies in her hair. "Spanish coin, Your Grace. There are hundreds of prettier girls here."

"Yes, but they all agree with everything I say. You don't. Just like my Sondra. That's true beauty. Did I ever tell you about . . ."

The viscount opened the hand that had held Sydney's in parting. He smiled when he saw the daisy there in his palm and nodded when he brought it to his lips. She was his. He could wait.

26

Bella of the Ball

It was going to be the best ball of the Season, or Sydney would die trying. She'd likely kill everyone else in the household, too, working so hard on decorations, foodstuffs, guest lists, the millions of details an undertaking of this proportion required. Sydney was in her element. The rest of her friends and family were in dismay.

Finally the invitations were all printed and delivered. General Harlan Lattimore, Ret., was proud to invite the world, they indicated, to witness the betrothal of his granddaughter Winifred to Brennan, son of, etc., on such a date. The engagement would be celebrated at a benefit ball, the proceeds enriching the War Veterans' Widows and Orphans Fund, with paid admission at the door and other donations gratefully accepted.

The invitations went out under the general's name, in Winifred's copperplate, with the duke's frank, at Sydney's instigation, according to the duchess. Nearly everyone accepted, even the Prince

Regent, who declared it a novel idea and Sydney an original.

Sydney did not have time to be anything but an organizer. There were measurements and fittings—for the rooms as well as the girls. Lists of guests, lists of supplies, lists of lists. Sydney met with musicians, caterers, hiring agencies. She heard out Aunt Harriet and took Lady Mayne's advice. The duchess was delighted, not just that she was preferred over that clutch-fisted Lady Windham, but that Sydney had such an aptitude. The minx would make a worthy duchess, if that scrod of a son of hers would get on with it.

The duchess had high hopes for the ball. There was nothing like the excitement of a fancy affair to bring a sparkle to a maiden's eyes, and nothing like seeing how popular a chit was to make a man take notice. Like her dogs with their toys, a favorite ball could lie untouched for days, but let one dog play with it, they all had to have it. Men were no different. Nothing would make a male claim possession quicker than others sniffing around his chosen mate. And the duchess intended them to sit up and howl. Her own dressmaker was in charge of the Lattimores' gowns; that was to be her betrothal gift. Winifred's dress was a delicate shell pink with a lace overskirt, selected to set off the ruby pendant the duchess knew Brennan intended to give her. But Sydney's dress was not going to be any sweet pastel or wedding-cake froth. It was a simple one-shouldered fall of watered blue-green silk that clung to her lush form and changed colors with movement and light, just like her eyes. With it she would wear a peacock-eye plume mounted on a gold fillet in her hair, gold sandals, and gold silk gloves.

If that didn't stir a declaration out of the sapskull, his doting mother vowed, she'd stir his brains with a footstool!

Sydney was too busy to worry about the viscount, but she knew what she knew, and smiled inside.

She was too busy for morning calls and such, but she made time for Bella, not wishing to appear to slur old friends, even when the duchess said Mrs. Ott reminded her of a housekeeper at some Irish hunt party.

Bella thought a benefit ball an excellent idea, especially when she heard the name of the charity. "Why, it's a sure stroke of genius, dearie, seeing how you're an orphan and I'm a widow. Ha-ha."

"I know you're only teasing, Mrs. Ott. You don't think anyone will suppose I am keeping the money, do you?"

"Stealing from the needy? Lawks, dearie, who'd ever think a thing like that?"

There would never be another ball like Sydney's. Decorations were joyous, with holly garlands and white satin bows draping the succession of rooms. Food was lavish, not confined to one refreshments area, but set up on tables in each room, with servants constantly circulating with wine and lemonade and champagne and trays of stuffed oysters and lobster patties and sweets. Music was everywhere, an orchestra in the large ballroom, a string quartet in a smaller reception room where sofas and comfortable chairs were placed, a gifted young man playing the pianoforte in the corner of another parlor. There was a card room with no music at all. There were candles and mirrors and a lantern-strung balcony, footmen to take the wraps, maids to repin hems and hairdos, majordomos to call out the names of the distinguished guests.

All of Sydney's careful planning was coming to glorious fulfillment, not just the details of the ball. Winifred was angelic in her happiness, Bren looking like the cat in the cream pot as they greeted each guest coming through the receiving line. The general was resplendent in his full-dress uniform, sword, medals, and sash, as he beamed proudly from his wheelchair between Winifred and Sydney. Aunt Harriet stood next on the line, formidable in magenta taffeta and ostrich feathers, her nose only slightly out of joint at having to pay admission. Not even family was exempt. The duchess stood nearby with her duke for a brief while, gloating. And the viscount had sent Sydney a gold filigree fan.

Best of all, the huge punch bowl in the entryway was filling up. Willy and Wally flanked the bowl like handsome bookends in their new red and white livery, exchanging party favors for the admission fee, boutonnieres of holly and white carnations for the gentlemen, dance cards on white satin ribbons for the ladies. As the delighted guests wandered around the rooms, some of them strolled back to congratulate the Lattimores again. They often dropped a stickpin or an earring or a snuffbox in the bowl, for such a good cause.

And the Prince did come for a brief, memorable moment. His equerry handed Willy a check, which everyone knew would be generous and not worth the paper it was writ on. Prinny did toss one of his rings in the bowl for the benefit of the poor families of those who gave their lives for God and country— and for the benefit of everyone who gathered in the reception area to see him. He smiled and waved as all the ladies in the room went into their deepest curtsies. Sydney's knees turned to pudding when he stopped in front of her after saying a few kind words to the general, then a firm hand was under her elbow, helping her wobbly knees lift the rest of her uncooperative body off the ground. Forrest was there next to her, and she could do anything, even smile at the heavy-handed flirtation of the heavy head of state.

Then it was time to start the dancing. The general was enjoying himself so much, smiling at old friends and accepting the well-wishes of old adversaries that Sydney asked if he wanted to stay on to greet latecomers.

"Go on, go on," Aunt Harriet scolded, "I'm paying those musicians by the night, not the song. I'll stay and see the old tartar doesn't fall off his seat or stab anyone with his sword."

Leaving Griffith behind the general's chair ready to wheel him away if he got tired, Sydney and Winifred went into the ballroom. The newly engaged couple led the opening cotillion and the duke and duchess followed, looking more in charity with each other than anyone could remember.

"Must be the season for love," one old dowager commented.

"Stuff," another replied, "they just ran out of reasons for fighting."

Then Forrest held his hand out to lead Sydney into the dance. There was not much chance for conversation in the pattern of the steps, but the touch of his hand brought a tingle she felt to her toes, and his smile almost filled her heart to bursting. The ball, the world, was a lifetime away. Soon, his eyes promised. But too soon it was time to trade partners and get back to being hostess. Sydney danced with the duke, Brennan, her own admirers, and some of Winifred's disappointed suitors, even Baron Scoville. Between dances she checked on the refreshments and the card room and the general in the entry hall.

Bella and her party arrived late. She kept her cloak with her, saying she was leaving early. She was not surprised to see Willy and Wally still near the door, for they were to stand there all night, guarding the punch bowl now gratifyingly full of donations. Bella handed over the price for two admissions.

"She's my new Indian maid," she told Willy, nodding toward the small woman draped in fabric who walked behind her. "She ain't going in, so I don't have to pay for her. This is for me and the captain." Bella's escort also tried to walk behind her. She dragged him to her side when she saw the general and Lady Windham, whom she had not expected to be where they were, not at all. While she was thinking, she yanked off one of her rings and tossed it in the bowl. "For the starving children." Let them eat paste.

Then she jerked the Indian girl forward and told the general, "This here's Ranshee. She'll stand here and look decorative for the folks. You can ask her to help; she understands English fine, don't you, Ranshee?"

The girl salaamed to the general, holding the edge of her veil across her face. Her eyes were darkened with kohl; her skin with tea. Her sari was yards of silk; two coffins were going naked into the earth.

The general had seen many an Indian maid in his day. Some even had hairy arms. None, however, had green eyes and wisps of red hair beneath their headpieces. Few were liable to have knives tucked in their sandals either. The general made his growling noises.

"Hush up, you old lecher," Lady Windham hissed in his ear. Griffith turned the general's chair away in case the sight of the Hindu girl was bringing back bad memories.

General Lattimore was now directly facing Bella's male escort, whom she introduced as Captain Otis Winchester. One of the naked coffins belonged to an officer of the Home Guard who went out for pistols for two, breakfast for one. He wasn't the one. Bella sewed an old shoe buckle over the heart-high rip, like another medal. The captain walked with a limp and a cane and had a patch over one eye. He also had a full beard and mustache and muttonchop sideburns, which were not all the exact same shade, but close enough. Like the general, he wore an ornamental sword and a sidearm pistol.

"One of our brave boys wounded in battle," Bella told the general, who promptly saluted, even though he couldn't quite make out the lad's rank and medals.

Bella had to kick the captain and whisper, "Salute, you dunderhead."

So Chester saluted. Ah, the old bar sinister, Chester's inheritance from his true father, was to have its day. Chester saluted with his left hand.

The general's face turned red. He gurgled in his throat and started pounding on his chair arm. Griffith wheeled him closer to the door for a little fresh air.

The Indian maid Ranshee, meanwhile, having taken up a serving tray from one of the waiters, went to offer an hors d'oeuvre to Lady Windham. Unfortunately the poor girl tripped over her sari and spilled the tray of hot lobster patties right down Lady Windham's magenta décolletage. One of the Minch twins came running over when the countess shrieked. Captain Winchester, praying the remaining footman was Willy of the fragile mandible, hit the fellow a resounding blow. It was Wally and he hit back, sending Chester's mustache flying in the general's direction. Griffith wheeled him around in time to see Bella pick up Winchester's cane and whap Wally over the head a few times until the footman went down. By now the Indian girl had torn off her veil and headpiece and was holding a knife to Willy's throat, or as close as pint-sized Randy could get. If that was Wally, though, this must be the easy one, so toothless Randy hit Willy alongside the jaw with the heavy silver tray. They got it right that time.

Aunt Harriet was flat on the ground in a swoon, like a banquet table for sea gulls. Bella was holding open her cloak while a groggy Chester tipped the donation bowl's contents into it.

When the bowl was empty, Bella knotted her cloak and headed for the door, Chester limping at her heels, Randy not far behind. But there was the general, cutting off retreat, his dress sword stretched in front of him, one last battle cry on his lips, his faithful batman wheeling him into the fray.

So the O'Toole tribe retrenched and headed for another exit, through the ballroom and out the glass doors to the rear gardens. In making her plans, Bella had not counted on finding half the upper ten thousand between her and escape. Sydney was first on the scene, having been headed in that direction anyway. Randy grabbed her before she could cry out, and held her in front of him as a shield, the knife now pressed to *her* throat. Bella lugged the sack and Chester limped, followed by Wally on his knees, and the general leading his own charge.

The moment they reached the ballroom, things got even more interesting. Ladies shrieked and fell into the arms of whoever was close by, even poor, homely men. Winnie started sobbing. Forrest and Brennan ran forward, but slid to a halt when they saw the knife threatening Sydney and the pistol now in Bella's hands. The viscount cursed when he reached for a sword that wasn't by his side. Those guests who were not trampling each other in their efforts to leave made sure there was a clear path to the doors. Then the duchess, standing by the refreshments table, saw her typically inept sons at a standstill and took matters into her own hands. A punch cup in one hand, a saucer in the other. Soon she was joined by the duke in an artillery fusillade that could have ended the Peninsular Wars years earlier. Bella's gun was shot out of her hands by a dish of raspberry ice.

"Good shot, my dear."

"Years of practice, darling."

Dodging and weaving, the trio with their burdens tried to progress. Hobble-footed Chester slipped on the broken crockery and went down under the barrage. He pulled himself up by his mama's skirts, even though she kicked him. She grabbed his pistol. The general and his faithful Sancho Panza finally made their way into the thick of things. The general's outthrust sword nicked Bella's cloak, sending coins and gewgaws all over the floor. Chester slipped again. Wally hurtled onto his back, followed by Brennan. Bella whipped around, the pistol in her hand and blood in her eyes. Forrest ran forward and Sydney shrieked "No" along with a hundred other voices.

"You. You're the one caused all this, you meddling bastard," Bella spat at him. "Now I'm going to kill you."

As cool as you please, Forrest held up a hand. "Just one question before you do, ma'am: Who the bloody hell are you?"

"I'm their ma, God help me," she snarled, and raised the gun. The crowd gasped. The duchess started heaving full cups, which only doused the onlookers cowering against the walls. Sydney, with a knife still to her throat, kicked and struggled and wept. And the general and Griff? They just kept coming. Not even the general could skewer a woman, in the back to boot, but he could boot her to kingdom come. He lowered his sword and raised his legs as Griffith gave a mighty shove.

The impact toppled the general and knocked Bella to the floor, but the gun went sailing. Everyone ducked and screamed, except Forrest, who fielded it neatly. "All right, you bastard, let her go."

Randy kept twisting and looking over his shoulder, making sure no old geezers in wheelchairs were coming up behind him. His arm around Sydney's neck, he dragged her closer to the doors.

"You god id wrong again, Mayne. Chedder'd the battard. And you won'd shood, nod when I've shtill god the girl."

"How far do you think you'll get?" the viscount

stalled. It took Randy so long to say his piece, anything could happen.

Sydney was getting a little tired of people pointing guns at her beloved, to say nothing of having a little redheaded man in a dress and no teeth hold a knife to her throat. So while he was busy trying to answer Forrest and watch his back, she put her head down and bit his arm as hard as she could. Then she turned around and practiced Willy's lesson in self-defense. Not the one about using a closed fist, the other one, which caused the seams of her gown to split at the knee. At the same time, the duke let fly with the half-full glass punch bowl, which missed Randy since he was already on the floor, and caught Forrest full in the chest, with bits of orange and lemon decking the halls along with the ivy.

Baron Scoville was heard to declare the whole thing a disgrace. Trixie replied with a slap that sent his toupee flying toward the orchestra, which immediately began playing *God Save the King*.

No, there would never be another ball like Sydney's.

27

Endings and Interest

"Dash it, Mischief, I didn't get to do anything! You saved yourself."

"Nonsense, you were very brave."

"No, I wasn't. I was terrified, seeing you in danger."

Sydney felt a sudden chill go through her at the thought of his facing Bella's pistol. She shuddered, but luckily she had something warm to fall back on, namely Forrest's chest.

They were back in Park Lane and it was nearly dawn. Her dress was changed, the vegetation was combed out of his hair, the O'Tooles long gone. They were most likely going to be transported, according to Bow Street. The reward money, it was decided, would go to the Minch brothers to open their inn. The duke and duchess were so in accord with each other and the world, they decided to match the ball's profits with a charitable donation of their own, which should scotch any rumors of misappropriation. Lord and Lady Mayne were so delighted with themselves, they even left Sydney and Forrest alone together, after getting a full explanation of events right back to Brennan's involvement.

The duke winked at Sydney on his way out, but told his son he better get a shrewd solicitor to handle the settlements. Sydney blushed, for nothing had been said about—

"Go on, you old windbag, let Forrest do things his own way," the duchess admonished, shooing her husband out the door. She was content now that Forrest would do it, but couldn't resist adding as she left, "Just one thing, my dears. That little dog of Sydney's? She's one of the best Pekingese in all of England, with a pedigree fancier than the Prince's by half."

"We really are not interested in dog stories, Mother. Not now." Forrest was just a trifle impatient.

"Of course you aren't, dear, but Sydney may be. I believe Princess Pennyfleur is breeding. The pups should fetch a pretty penny indeed."

Sydney's eyes lit up, and she would have followed the duchess out the door, except for Forrest's hand on her arm, pulling her back to the sofa.

"I still cannot believe that of Bella," Sydney mused while Forrest added another log to the fire.

"I don't see why you don't believe it. I would never call you a fine judge of character, Mischief. Just think how you used to believe I was the lowest scum on earth." He sat next to her on the couch, pulling her closer.

She went willingly, but complained, "Well, you used to think I was a hopeless hoyden."

"But I was right, Mischief," he told her, blowing feathery kisses on her curls, "you are."

Sydney giggled. "Do you think I'll ever be invited anywhere again?"

"They'll never refuse a someday duchess." Now he was kissing her ear and the side of her neck.

"A . . . someday . . . duchess?"

"A current viscountess will have to do, then. A marriage will stop all the gossip instantly, you know. Will you?"

Sydney sat up and drew away. "Just to stop the gossip?" she asked indignantly.

"No, you goose," he laughed, pulling her into his lap. "To stop my heart from breaking. I have loved you from the first minute I saw you, despite myself, and I cannot bear to be without you a day longer. If I offered you my heart and my hand, do you think you could return my affection just a little?"

"Just a little? Is that all you want?"

"No, sweetheart, I want you to love me as I love you, with my very soul."

"I always have. I'll love you back with my heart and my soul, forever and ever, a hundred times over for all you love me. No, a thousand."

Which is a pretty fair rate of interest on any loan.